Ruthless and Rotten:

Say U Promise 2

Ruthless and Rotten:

Say U Promise 2

Ms. Michel Moore

www.urbanbooks.net

Urban Books, LLC
97 N18th Street
Wyandanch, NY 11798

ISBN 13: 978-1-62286-934-3
ISBN 10: 1-62286-934-6

First Trade Paperback Printing November 2014
First Mass Market Printing December 2015
Printed in the United States of America

10 9 8 7 6 5 4 3 2 1

*This is a work of fiction. Any references or sim-
ilarities to actual events, real people, living or
dead, or to real locales are intended to give the
novel a sense of reality. Any similarity in other
names, characters, places, and incidents is entire-
ly coincidental.*

Distributed by Kensington Publishing Corp.
Submit Wholesale Orders to:
Kensington Publishing Corp.
C/O Penguin Group (USA) Inc.
Attention: Order Processing
405 Murray Hill Parkway
East Rutherford, NJ 07073-2316
Phone: 1-800-526-0275
Fax: 1-800-227-9604

1

OLD NEWS

Fatima and Brother Rasul drove both of the girls to the airport so they could catch the red-eye flight. They said their farewells at the gate and sadly boarded the Texas-bound aircraft.

"Don't worry, London. You'll be safe when we get to Dallas. Storm and his boy Deacon have got that town on lock! We gonna be good!"

Kenya was trying endlessly to ease her sister's troubled mind, while she herself was a hot, nervous wreck. When they landed and got their luggage, Kenya tried calling Storm's cell phone, but unfortunately, once again it went straight to voice mail. Needless to say, she was starting to get beyond worried.

"Damn, why isn't his ass answering? He'd better not be fucking around with one of those island Bitches!" Kenya slyly mumbled under her breath.

"Is everything all right?" London asked her sister as she looked directly in Kenya's face.

She could tell that it was a problem. Even Ray Charles could.

"Yeah, I was just trying to call Storm. He must not be back in town yet, but it ain't a big deal. I'm straight!"

Kenya didn't know how she was going to break the news to him about London. After all, she had been lying. Well, sort of. He always thought her uncle was the only family that she had, but bottom line it was time for her to face the music. Storm didn't have a choice in the matter. He would have to accept London and she, in return, would have to accept Storm and his crooked lifestyle.

Kenya tried not to worry as the pair took a taxi to her and Storm's condo. When they drove up, Kenya noticed all the lights on inside the house. She then made a mental note to curse Storm out for leaving all the lights on. He was, after all, the main one complaining about the bills.

"Well, this is it! I can't wait for you to see how I decorated it!" Kenya excitedly leaped out the cab, stretching her arms.

"So this is it, huh?" London looked around the quiet street that her sister had been calling home.

The driver sat the bags on the curb, waited for his tip, and pulled off into the darkness of the night. Kenya and London picked them up slowly and made their way up to the door.

"Wait 'til you see it, London. It is nice as hell. It's everything I've ever dreamed about." Kenya stuck her key in the door, strangely discovering it was unlocked. *He must have really been in a rush.* Confused as to why Storm had carelessly left without securing their home, Kenya pushed the door wide opened and stepped inside the entranceway. *What the fuck!* She couldn't believe her eyes and what she and her sister were faced with. "Oh, my God! Oh, my God! Oh *nooooo!*" Kenya almost collapsed to the floor as London held her chest in utter disbelief. The karma that Kenya had put out in the universe had just come back to bite her dead in the ass!

2

Welcome Home

Kenya and London stood in somewhat of a daze. It was like looking at something out of a movie. London was totally confused, while her sister was completely shaken up. Both girls simultaneously turned, glimpsing over their shoulders to see if they could try to stop the cabdriver, who just dropped the two of them off. Unfortunately for the pair, he had already pulled down the block. Undoubtedly on his way back to the airport in search of another fare for the night, the girls were all alone and on their own. The only thing they could make out was his brake lights as he slowed down, bending the corner of the quiet gated community that Kenya and Storm called home.

"Oh, my God! Oh, my God! Oh shit!" a stunned Kenya repeated in a loud, panic-filled voice, standing in the threshold. "I'll be damned! What in the hell happened in this place? Storm! Storm! Oh, my God. Storm—where you at?"

"Wow—what happened here?" London quizzed, dumbfounded and astonished.

Kenya yelled out her fiancé's name once more, as her twin sister London's jaw fell open, almost dropping to the ground. "I can't believe this bullshit!" Her eyes were stretched open wide and soon filled with tears as she quickly glanced around her once-perfect, gorgeously designed living room. "Storm! Storm!" she shrieked, still standing frozen in the doorway with her knees weakening by the second and her lips trembling from fear. "This is a nightmare, London. I'm confused!"

"Kenya, what went on in here? How did this occur?" London wondered, interrupting her sister's apparent emotional breakdown. "This is awful. I mean—wow!"

The pair couldn't believe their own eyes, let alone stomach the nauseating, eye-stinging stench that caused them to almost throw up. London, not knowing what else to expect, reached over, grabbing her sister's hand tightly as they hesitantly made their way completely into the high-priced condo. Leaving the custom-carved wooden door unlocked and open just in case they needed to make a quick escape, they each prayed for the best. Considering what the pair had just been through back home in Detroit and the overall condition of the room, neither Kenya nor London knew what to expect with each passing step that they took.

It was burning hot inside the condo. Kenya raised her hand to the thermostat, turning off the heat that was strangely on full blast, like Miami. The temperature had caused the walls to sweat and each girl to immediately become drenched in perspiration. As the seconds past, it was becoming painstakingly clear something was drastically wrong. First, all the lights in the house being left turned on, then the heating system on the nut, and of course, her living room destroyed. What else was next? What else could possibly go wrong? Kenya was beyond terrified and needed her man by her side, not her scary cat and judgmental sister.

"Storm! Baby, are you here?" she pleaded repeatedly, hoping for a response. "Are you at home? Please answer me, baby—please!"

London darted her eyes around her twin's supposedly new home. She looked at the huge painting hanging over the fireplace that was crooked and peeling away from the frame. Next, she focused her sights onto the obviously dam-aged wine-colored leather furniture, as well as the completely destroyed, crushed coffee table. Despite the terrible mildew odor that filled the room and the mess that surrounded them, London could tell that Kenya once had the condo organized and magazine worthy, but now was not the time to complement her on her style or flare for fashion.

The newly laid, plush wall-to-wall white carpet was now soiled with debris. It was soaked with filthy water turning some areas dark brown. The soles of the girls' shoes were wet, submerging deep into the carpet, making squishing sounds with each step. Sections of the ceiling were caved in, exposing the floor support beams of the upstairs rooms, along with a constant stream of water still causing chaos.

"Listen sis, seriously, from the look of things it seems as if your so-so brain-challenged, brilliant boyfriend must have left the water running somewhere in the house. He must be the smartest man alive. Kenya girl, you are so lucky to have a man like him." London snickered at her twin, shaking her head. "We need to at least get the water turned off!"

"Damn London, college did teach ya li'l behind one thing!" Kenya put her hand on her hip, definitely not in the mood. "To be a real smart-ass!" She wiped the dripping sweat off her forehead, rolled her eyes, and waved her hand in London's face. "And FYI, he's not my boyfriend! Remember the ring! Remember this here ring, heffa! My man put a ring on it for real!"

The tension that was originally felt when they walked into the condo was broken briefly by the girls clowning on one another.

"Okay, 'Miss I Got The Ring', why don't you go upstairs and see where all this water is coming from. I'll try to open some of these windows and let some fresh air in here. I can hardly breathe in this palace of yours."

"You mean you want me to go up those stairs all by myself?" Kenya pouted with her lips stuck out. "You must be insane or something! I don't know what's up them damn stairs!"

London laughed at her sister. "You so big and bad all the time, thinking you can beat the world! Why don't you go by ya dang-gone self? Who stopping you?"

"Stop playing around so much and come on." Kenya yanked her sister by the shoulder. Arm in arm, they both slowly headed toward the staircase.

The closer they crept to the top of the condo stairs, they could clearly hear the sounds of water running. The floor on the upper level was much more damaged than the downstairs, causing the twins to lean on each other for support so they wouldn't slip or fall. The horrible smell that'd taken over the living room was getting worse. The water that drenched the carpet was more infested with debris than the bottom of the condo.

"It must've been the fish tank that overflowed," Kenya finally reasoned with herself, trying to calm her nerves. She started feeling somewhat relieved at the thought all this bullshit she'd been met with on her return home was nothing more than an unfortunate accident. "That's the only water that could be flowing from that direction. Maybe the pump broke or something. That has to be some of Storm's dead fish or something like that." She waved her hand across her nose.

"Yeah, you're probably right, Kenya. That's got to be it. I mean, that's the only reasonable explanation for this ratchet smell." Using the collar of her shirt as a mask, London rolled her eyes. As they got to the edge of the slightly cracked den door, pushing it wide open, the odor worsened. The smothering heat that was trapped inside rushed out and hit them smack dead in the face. "Oh dang gee! It smells like not some, but all your fish are already dead." London twisted her face, turning up her lip. "God it smells bad! *Urggg*, I wanna throw up! Yuk!"

"All right girl—damn! Stop with all the dramatics and carrying on! I know it stank bad as hell, but listen, I'm gonna run in my bedroom and get the telephone number to the condo management so they can send someone out here ASAP. You go in and at least see if any of them are still alive." Kenya tightly placed her hand over her nose and mouth, hoping to stop the overpowering stench from filling her throat. "I'll be right back. Shit! Storm is gonna be pissed the hell off. He put a lot of dough into that freaking aquarium." She left her sister standing in the hallway as she disappeared into her bedroom.

This is so dang-gone gross, London thought, walking into the unfamiliar room, searching the wall for the light switch. She felt the side of her tan Payless loafers being filled with water she could only assume was contaminated. Carefully, she bent down to roll up her pants legs that were dragging along the floor, making each step much grimier than the last. "Kenya, is you gonna replace my shoes! Cheap or not—I just bought these!" She angrily barked out, hoping her sister heard her declaration. The fish tank was located over on the far left side of the spacious room. It was making a terrible piercing, grinding sound. She wanted to place her hands on her ears to block some of the annoying noise, but would have to stop using her collar as a mask. At this point the smell was worse than the sound, so she chose to endure the lesser of two evils. London slowly headed over to investigate the huge fish tank and hopefully solve the source of the problem.

Kenya made it to the side of her and Storm's king-sized bed. Disgusted at what kind of cleanup she was facing, she sat down on the edge of the mattress. Opening the nightstand drawer, she grabbed the business-card flyer with all the condo management's contact numbers on it. As she quickly scanned down the list, she overheard the sound of more water flowing from one of the adjoining bathrooms.

The two baths that were connected from the master bedroom were designed differently to fit both her and Storm's own individual taste. Kenya's was old-fashioned, with a sink and tub that was porcelain with antique-inspired fixtures. It reminded her of her grandmother's house, a place she'd always love. On the other hand, Storm's private bathroom had a shower that had a beveled three-color glass door and a sunken, custom-designed walk-in tub that could comfortably fit at least two people without a problem.

I know Storm's crazy self ain't leave the water on in his precious bathroom! He better not have! Kenya huffed, thinking to herself as she leaped to her feet, bolting into the bathroom. *If he did, then that's his ass! I swear on everything that's in his pockets! He got my entire house on the nut smelling and looking like God-knows-what!*

When Kenya ran inside, she immediately lost her balance from all the water spewed across the marble floor. Not able to catch herself from falling, she slid, scraping her arm and shoulder on the way down. "Ain't this a bitch," she mumbled angrily, soaked to her skin. "Now my clothes are ruined and shit! He's gonna straight-up replace my outfit! Trust and believe! Who does this—who? First, he leaves the heat blasting on hell, lets the fish tank run over, now this! Where they do that at?"

Sure enough, she quickly realized the water was indeed turned on full speed in the tub and had overflowed. The room smelled just like raw, dirty rotten sewage. Kenya, nauseated, was almost in tears again as she tried getting up and slipped back down in all the muck. Instead of attempting to walk over to shut the water off, she wisely decided to crawl. At this point, it would be much easier than trying to stand up. So, on her hands and knees, drenched, slimy, and covered in God-knows-what, Kenya cursed the love of her life as she tried to maintain her composure through the turmoil.

"I'm gonna flat-out kill that fool Storm when I see him. How could he be so careless? This is ridiculous!"

London cautiously neared the corner of the room. Not able to move, she started to hyperventilate at the sight of the huge aquarium and what was seemingly inside. Her entire body was shaking uncontrollably and she became lightheaded. She opened her mouth to yell out her sister's name, but no sound was coming out. Terrified, London grasped for air, holding her chest while backing up slowly.

"*Kenyaaaaa! . . . Kenyaaaaa!*" she stuttered loudly, finally getting the words together. "Come here quick! Hurry up! Please hurry!" London's heart was pounding and seemed as if it was going to jump out her body. With her adrenaline racing, the once naive-to-life college student bolted out the room. Fighting to make sense of what she'd just seen, she stumbled into the debris-covered hallway. Her system broke all the way down. She couldn't hold back any longer. Disgusted beyond belief, London threw up all over herself and the already filth-soiled carpet. "Kenya! Kenya!" Gagging, she continued to call out while wiping her mouth with the sleeve of her shirt.

London's repeated shouts of fear were interrupted by a constant assault of Kenya's high-pitched screams. Desperate to reunite with her twin, she followed the sound of her sister's voice down the hall, in the bedroom, and lastly into the bathroom. "Kenya! Kenya! Please—you have to hurry and come with me," London shouted loudly. "You need to see this! Matter of fact—we need to get out of here!"

Focused on revealing what she'd seen, London rushed inside the bathroom. Painfully, she had the same misfortune as Kenya, sliding across the floor past the sink and toilet, landing flat on her back. London, still frightened, half out her mind, was now next to a sobbing, also scared and in shock, Kenya, who couldn't do anything but point her trembling finger. Placing both hands down on the cold, dirty, and wet marble floor, London sat up and reached for her twin. "What is it Kenya? What are you trying to say? What is it?"

No words came out her otherwise tough-natured sister's mouth as she continued to point. Not knowing what to expect in this surprising house of horrors, London took a deep breath, preparing herself for more of the unknown. Leaning over, she bravely peeked over into the bathtub, taking a long, hard stare. Astonished once again, London felt as if she and Kenya were costarring in a bad, low-budget scary movie, considering all the bad luck that was following them around.

3

Oh Shit!

"Who is this, Kenya?" a shocked London demanded to know after seeing a body floating in the tub. "Do you know this man? Kenya, is this your boyfriend? Is it?"

Kenya was hysterical and trembling. In a trancelike state, she seemed not to comprehend anything that her sister was asking. The unthinkable was now happening to them all over again: another dead body at their feet. After crawling through the toxic mess and leaning over to turn the knob, London found the totally nude, dead, decaying, bloated body ass-up underwater. And to make matters even more horrible, it had been decapitated.

"Please, Kenya. Listen to me!" London grabbed her twin's shoulders, shaking her hard. "Kenya, do you hear me? Listen—you've got to snap out of it! It might be somebody still in here. We need to get out of this place and call the police ASAP! Kenya—listen!"

London was getting no response from a zombielike Kenya and could only think of one thing to do. So, with one of her wet hands, London raised back with all her strength and knocked the cow-walking shit out of her. *Smack!* The sound was so loud it instantly woke Kenya up out her trance. London rubbed her stinging hand and repeated her first question. "Now, is this Storm? Is this your boyfriend?"

"Naw, sis. Naw, that's not him. Oh, my God—I'm not sure who that is!" a red-faced Kenya screamed, somehow making it to her feet and running out the bathroom, back into the bedroom. Instinctively she rushed over to the closet, getting one of the many guns that were stashed all around the condo. Wanting to protect herself as well as London, she put one up top. "I don't know what the hell is going on. I need to find Storm! He'll know what to do! This is crazy! This whole thing is crazy!"

London was hot on her sister's heels and kept the questions coming one after another. "Kenya—we should get out of here! We should call the damn police! And are you sure that isn't Storm?" London stared at Kenya, waiting for the answer.

"Dang, what in the hell is wrong with you? Are you crazy? I just said that ain't Storm in there!" Kenya was getting pissed about this nightmare she was caught up in and all the unanswered questions that were coming along with it. "Don't you think I know my own man, London, head or no head?"

"Well?" London replied. "What are you waiting for? We need to call the police!

"Forget calling the damn cops! You must be out ya rabbit-ass mind! And just how would we explain this bullshit, a mysterious body floating in the tub with the freaking head missing?"

Pulling her by the arm, London forced her angry, now gun-carrying twin out the bedroom, down the hallway. "Come with me, Kenya. I need to show you something that might help you figure out exactly who that could be floating in your tub."

As the pair cautiously walked into the den, Kenya, urged by her twin, gradually eased over to the noisy fish tank and got a good look.

"What the—! Oh hell naw!" The once–strong-minded female was standing face-to-face with a head submerged in the corner of the aquarium. Its eyes were half eaten and mutilated by the few larger-than-normal fish that were still alive, swimming in and out of its mouth. Weak in the knees, Kenya was seconds away from passing out. A familiar letter-A, custom-designed yellow diamond earring was barely glistening through the dirty water. She recognized it immediately as one of three that she, Deacon, and Storm wore religiously to represent their club, Alley Cats. Kenya clutched her chest, falling back over toward the doorway and falling into her sister's arms. Confused, she shivered with fear and total, chaotic uncertainty. "Why? Why? I don't understand!"

"Do you know him, Kenya—do you? Is that Storm?" London once again coldly drilled, talking over the piercing sound that still filled the air. "Is it?"

"Damn bitch! What the fuck is wrong with you?" Kenya snatched away, ready to attack her own blood. "Naw, that ain't no motherfucking Storm! Now stop asking me that dumb shit and acting so stupid!"

London knew that Kenya was in shock, so she let all of her disrespectful comments go without firing back her own round of insults. "Well, who is it, then? Do you know? Can you recognize him?"

"Yeah, I know." Kenya's face was full of sorrow and regret. She remorsefully dropped her head down, holding the huge gun tightly in her small hand. "It's Storm's best friend—his boy Deacon. They were supposed to be together when they left town." Kenya started to let her tears pour. "But if they left town, why is Deacon here? And where is Storm?"

"Wow!" London shook her head in disbelief. "Listen, sis, enough of this bizarre madness we going through. We need to first get out of here and secondly call the police!"

"I'm scared, London! I'm really, really scared!"

London hugged her twin, trying her best to console her. "We need to call the police, Kenya." She placed both hands on her sister's shoulder, looking her dead in the eyes. "We need some help. I mean, seriously, what kind of folk do you know in this awful town who would do something so heinous like this? And are you sure they're not coming back or worst than that, still in here somewhere! What kinda people you deal with?"

"Yeah right!" Kenya judgmentally looked at London with a dumb expression and replied. "Probably the same assholes who were trying to get at you for that P.A.I.D. bullshit you so insistent with organizing! That's the only people I can think of. Now, how about that?" Kenya still found it hard to believe this was happening to her; to them. "But who would do something as treacherous as cut off a human's head? What have you done? Who you done pissed off with those speeches of yours?"

"Yeah all right, maybe I do have some enemies, but I don't understand. What in the world would your boyfriend's friend have to do with me and my personal business?" London fired back, folding her arms.

"Who knows?" Kenya wiped her tears away, trying to regain her composure. "But one thing is for sure. It's no way in hell we can call the cops to find out that answer. We definitely can't do that!"

"Okay then, Kenya. What's the game plan? We gotta do something—I mean, it's a dead body in your bathtub and a head over there! I vote for calling the damn police!"

"Look, I'm gonna call O.T. He'll know what we should do and hopefully he's heard from Storm."

"Who is O.T.?"

"That's my man's little brother. He's running Alley Cats for Deacon and Storm while they're out of town."

"And what in the world is Alley Cats?" London quizzed as things grew weirder by the moment.

"That's the strip club that Deacon and Storm own. They're partners."

"Well, sis," she pointed at the aquarium that was still loud before pulling the plug out the wall socket. "I guess you mean the club that Storm owns now. Don't you?"

"Damn, London, that's some real fucked-up shit to say right about now!" Kenya glanced at the bedroom door, getting chills thinking about Deacon's headless floating body, as they passed on the way downstairs. "But, yeah, I guess you're right. It is Storm's now."

London shrugged her shoulders, following her sister out onto the front porch. They moved their luggage to the side of the door and sat on the bottom stair. Kenya, praying for the best, pulled out her cell.

"I've gotta make this call to O.T., so we can get some damn help!" Kenya nervously fumbled with her phone.

"Okay, I know he's Storm's brother, but what is he, a detective or something? I mean . . ." London questioned her twin, wondering what was coming next. "Can he help with a headless corpse in a tub? Just what kind of people are you out here affiliating with?"

"Damn, London, damn! Stop asking me all of them questions and let me make this fucking call! Damn!"

"Okay, okay, sorry to annoy you! Go ahead and call him."

With her heart beating overtime, Kenya nervously dialed O.T.'s number. After about four or five rings, Storm's grumpy-voiced brother answered.

4

What Da Hell

"Yeah, speak on it!" O.T. was angry and pissed off by being disturbed from his sleep. "And you better make the shit quick, fast, and in a hurry with your words!"

"Hey O.T., this is Kenya."

"I know who it is," he barely mumbled. "What you want so damn early in the morning? A nigga like me just got in the bed good and shit."

"I was wondering, have you talked to Storm yet?" Kenya held her breath, waiting for his response. She prayed to God that he would say yes.

"That's why you called me?" O.T. shouted through the phone, loud enough for London to hear. "You blowing up my phone because you can't catch up with dude? You set tripping like that? Come on now, Kenya, that's straight-up foul!" He was fed up with her and her constant calls.

"O.T., listen, I swear I'm sorry to wake you up, but this is a real emergency. Now, have you spoken to him or not?"

Sensing the seriousness in her attitude, he finally answered. "Naw, girl I ain't. What's wrong? What's the deal? I ain't talked to him or Deacon since they left."

"Oh, my God!" Kenya closed her eyes, crying softly as she lowered her head.

"*Oh, my God* what?" O.T. sat up in the bed and started to panic. "What the fuck is wrong, Kenya—what?"

Kenya's voice was cracking as she spoke. "I need you to come over here as soon as possible! I mean right damn now! For real, O.T., now!"

"What the fuck is wrong, Kenya?" he repeated, putting bass in his tone. "Stop playing around with me and let me know!"

A sound-asleep Paris, under the thin blanket lying next to O.T., immediately jumped up, startled by his loud, boisterous demands. "Who is that?" she mouthed the words. "What's going on? What's wrong? It better not be no bitch!"

"Chill on all that. It's Kenya! Something is wrong and shit!" O.T. was fuming as he shook his head at his girl and her always jealous behavior. He quickly turned his attention back to the phone conversation with Kenya. "Listen, can you cut the games out and give a brother a damn clue? Do I need to bring some fire over there or what? What's the deal?"

"I can't tell you over the phone," Kenya hysterically whined. "I need for you to just come over here now. Hurry, it's on a nine-one-one tip—real talk!"

"Okay, dig that. I'm on my way, Kenya! Just sit tight!"

Asking God for strength, she closed her cell phone, dropping her head once more. The reality of the situation was setting in for Kenya. This was a living nightmare she was trapped in. O.T. had just confirmed that Deacon and Storm had indeed left town together. Now she couldn't get in touch with her man, his brother hadn't heard from him, the condo was destroyed, and poor Deacon was dead as a doorknob. Whatever the explanation was could only mean trouble.

O.T. and Paris pulled up in front of the condo doing damn near a hundred miles per hour, certainly waking a neighbor or two. Paris slammed down hard on the brakes of her triple-black Chrysler 300M, causing the tires to come to a screeching, sudden halt. Leaping out the car before it came to a complete stop, O.T. ran up the walkway to see Kenya sobbing and another girl with her arm around her. By the time he got closer, the other girl raised her face, with its troubled expression, to meet his.

"What the fuck!" He had a puzzled look on his face as he turned back and forth, staring at both females sitting on the stairs. "Who the fuck?" O.T. shook his head in disbelief as Paris made her way to the group.

"Kenya? What the hell?" Paris, now totally bewildered, also questioned her best friend. "I don't understand."

"Yeah, who you telling? Me either!" O.T. raised his eyebrows. "This is straight wild!" The couple looked like they'd both seen a ghost.

Kenya stood up, wiping her face, leaving her twin sitting on the stair. "Hey, Paris. Hey, O.T. I know y'all confused and I'm gonna explain all of it later, I promise, but something awful done happened."

O.T., like Paris, couldn't take his eyes off of London. He was listening to the words come out of Kenya's mouth, but was in a daze trying to put two and two together. This was some *Twilight Zone*–type of bullshit to him.

"Y'all, this is my twin sister, London. She lives back out east in Detroit," Kenya quickly explained. "She's gonna stay with me and Storm for a little while."

"You got a twin? All this time and you didn't tell me? I thought we was way better than that!"

Paris felt insulted and betrayed by her best friend. "What was the big hush-hush secret?" she asked, while taking her time giving London the once-over.

"Ain't this some shit! Do my brother know about this?" O.T. threw both his arms up in the air in a harsh rage. "Damn, Kenya! Your ass is straight-up out of order! You must be on crack or something! It's been one thang after another with you! And what's all this mess on you? Damn, you stank!"

London sat with a stern expression of amazement at the two strangers who were supposed to be helping the nerve-racking situation give her sister the third degree.

"Listen, O.T . . . I—" Kenya tried her best to defend her deceitful actions before he continued speaking, stopping her in mid-sentence.

"Matter of fact, I know motherfucking well this ain't the damn emergency?" He spit on the grass and raised one of his tan-colored, untied Timberland boots onto the step next to London's leg.

Kenya's filthy fingers rubbed her forehead before moving strands of hair behind her ear. "Damn y'all, I know I was wrong for not mentioning it, but—"

"But what?" Paris, like O.T. had just done, cut her off. "You forgot? It slipped your mind all the times we done hung out?"

London was also completely thrown off that her own identical twin sister had somehow conveniently chose not to acknowledge her very existence to these people whom she had been living with for months. She would surely deal with that hurtful issue later, but for the time being, London had enough of them beating up her sister with all the questions and stepped in to intervene.

"I'm very sorry that you two supposed friends seem to have some sort of a gigantic problem with her having family out in this big world, but I think there's a much larger dilemma that we all have to deal with back in there." Covered in smelly muck on her hands and face, she rolled her eyes, pointing toward the cracked front door.

London's first impression of Kenya's friends and so-called great life was not very impressive, to say the least. Ready to discover the real reason for the late-night call, O.T. and Paris followed the twins into the destroyed home. Pulling their shirts over their noses to shield the overwhelming, eye-stinging stench, they both started to sweat.

"What the hell happened in this bitch?" O.T. frowned as he reached in his waistband, snatching out his pistol.

Paris was stunned, staying close to O.T. when she saw the awful condition inside the condo that Kenya had just remodeled.

"Come on upstairs, O.T." Kenya sighed. "That's the real and true problem."

"What's up there?" he grilled before bracin' up on the grip of his shiny, chrome-handled 9 mm. "What other crazy stuff you got going on?"

"It's not like that!" Kenya begged her fiancé's brother. "Please, just come with me. I couldn't explain what's up there for a million dollars. Plus, if I tried you wouldn't believe me anyhow! So just come on."

O.T. turned to go with Kenya. "Okay, girl, let's roll!" Paris was right behind him.

"You should stay down here with me," London suggested to her, gently grabbing her by the arm. "It's nothing that you would want to remember."

There was no need for Paris to have to see firsthand the dreadful, outrageous sight of Deacon's badly tortured body, let alone the whole aquarium thing with the floating head. London knew for a fact she wished she didn't have to live with the horrid memory or sleepless nights the flashback of it would bring.

Kenya sympathetically looked at her friend, urging her that London was 100 percent right. It would be much better for her to stay in the living room or what was left of it. Paris hesitantly agreed, standing silent next to London on the soaking wet carpet. As they watched Kenya and

O.T. navigate their way up the staircase, London got a slight chill in the muggy living room in anticipation of what Kenya and him were about to encounter.

"What's up there?" Paris broke the ice out of curiosity, staring at London, then at the caved-in ceiling. "Can you at least tell me? Clue a sista in! And damn, y'all look just the hell alike!"

"Trouble!" London replied, glancing up toward the stairs, trying to remain calm. "A lot of trouble!"

"Okay Kenya, we up here. Now what in the hell is the big surprise you got for me other than the living room is tore up?"

"You'll see, O.T., just follow me." Kenya led him down the hallway into her and Storm's bedroom.

"Urggh . . . dang! The smell is getting worse!" Still holding his gun tightly, he looked down at his new boots that were now ruined from all the water.

"It's in there." Kenya had broken down into tears as she nodded toward the bathroom door. "Go see for yourself. I'll be out here. I can't go back in there—not now. And be careful. It's extremely slippery on that floor." She wanted him to go in there alone and check it out. There was absolutely no desire for her to want to see Deacon in that state ever again.

"Oh shit! Oh fuck! Hell naw!" Kenya could hear O.T. stomping his feet, yelling at the top of his lungs as the water on the floor splashed. "What the fuck happened? Oh, hell naw! Kenya! Kenya!" He ran into the bedroom, where she was standing with a face full of flowing tears. "Where's his fucking head! Who the hell did this to my peoples?" O.T. was confused and running around the room from side to side. "Where is my fucking brother? Tell me, Kenya! Tell me!" O.T. demanded, snatching her up by the collar. "Where the fuck is he at?"

Kenya was having trouble breathing as she unsuccessfully struggled to get loose from his strong grip. "You're hurting me, O.T," she managed to say. "Let me go—please."

Shaking off his initial shock, he came back to earth and apologized. "Damn, Kenya, I'm sorry, but this shit is foul. I don't know what the fuck is going on here." He walked away from her and looked back in the bathroom once more to make sure he had truly seen what he thought he'd seen. "Where that guy's dome at and what about my brother? Is he in here too—in the house? Please tell me he ain't!" He dropped his head, swallowing extra hard, holding his gun down at his side as he paced. The wrong answer would cause him to bug all the way out.

"Naw, O.T., I haven't heard from him ever since I flew back home to Detroit. I've been calling his cell phone day after day and it keeps going straight to voice mail. That's why I kept calling you."

A relieved O.T. raised his face to look at Kenya dead on. "Do you know what went down here?"

"Nope—I don't. Me and my sister came home and the house was just like this." Kenya blew her nose with one of Storm's winter-white wife beaters that were lying across the bed. "The bottom was messed up and we heard water running. When we got up here to see where the water was coming from, I found Deacon's body in there."

"I can't believe this bullshit!" O.T. put his gun back in his waistband. "Whoever did that shit is ruthless as hell! Where's dude's hat rack at anyhow? Do you know?"

Kenya and he stepped out into the heavy-odor–filled hallway. "Go down there in the den and look in Storm's the fish tank."

"Yeah, right!" O.T. frowned, dialing his brother's cell number. "Come on now, Kenya! I know you gotta be bullshittin'!"

"I'm not playing. I'm serious. Go see for yourself. I wouldn't joke about something like that—not now."

"This is wild!" O.T. took in all the damage done in the condo as he walked in the den door with his cell phone up to his ear. By the time he came out, he was sweating bullets and fanning his hand in front of his face.

Paris and London were waiting at the end of the stairs as Kenya and O.T. came into view.

"What was it?" Paris grilled her man, noticing he was looking overly distressed. "Is it bad? Tell me! What was up there? What did you see?"

"Yeah, shit is fucked—really, really fucked up!" He softly touched Paris on her cheek. "We gotta figure this mess out quick and get in touch with my brother!"

All the girls stood silent in anticipation of what O.T., a known screwup and hot-tempered personality, had in store. Out of the two brothers, he was no doubt the irresponsible one. That was pretty much common knowledge with anyone who came in contact with them both. Kenya knew firsthand O.T. was a flat-out fool, but for now, he was her only hope of trying to retrace Storm and Deacon's last few days. She and he took turns blowing up Storm's cell phone in hopes that he would pick up and shed some sort of a light on all this madness.

While they waited, hoped, and prayed, O.T. and the three girls sat down on the stairs of the porch, coming up with a scheme to try to get Deacon's body and head out the crib. Until one of them talked to Storm and knew exactly what the deal was, they thought it would be much better to keep Deacon's brutal murder on the down-low. If the shit hit the fan out in the streets that Deacon was dead and Storm was missing, it would be sheer pandemonium. The different crews around town would think it would be their chance to try to take over drug territory that Storm and his fellas had worked so hard to pump up.

O.T. had no thoughts of blessing them with that golden opportunity. That meant the four of them, a skeptical London included, would be on their own in this awful mess. Repeatedly getting her fiancé's voice mail was causing a red-eyed Kenya to have a nervous breakdown from worry as the anxiety built. Trying to remain positive, her heart broke a little bit each passing second he didn't call back.

"What could have gone wrong? This just ain't right," O.T. wondered out loud, as he had Kenya collecting every sheet and blanket she could find. "As soon as we get this body up out of here, I'm gonna call that ho-ass nigga Royce and see what he know. He was supposed to be with Deacon and Storm when they left town. I know that old wannabe pimp know something—he gotsta to!"

Taking matters into his own hands, he knew he had to do the majority of the dirty work. As much as fearless street soldiers he knew his woman Paris and Kenya were, a headless body and a chopped-off head of a dude they had just partied with would be too much for the average man to stomach, let alone two females. O.T. drained all the water out the bathtub as well as the aquarium. Deacon's torso was bloated, stiff, and waterlogged, making it feel almost three times its normal body weight. Putting on two pairs of the rubber gloves that Paris had ran and bought from the corner store, he tried lifting Deacon up by himself, but it was no use. O.T. then instructed an extremely reluctant London and an eager-to-please Paris to put on gloves to help him. They both quickly came to his aid, knowing this was no time to argue. He then yelled out for his soon-to-be sister-in-law, but by that time the usually scared-of-nothing Kenya was, understandably, of no fucking good to any of them or herself. The once good girl turned all the way bad, was curled up on the edge of the bed, rocking back and forth with one of her beloved Storm's shirts in her arms.

The newly formed trio moved on with O.T.'s plan, wrapping the body first in a sheet, then in two fluffy comforters. Paris luckily found several old telephone cords out of the utility closet so they could tie Deacon snug. London had located a box of heavy-duty Home Depot garbage bags, which she doubled up. Holding the bags wide open, she turned away as O.T. dropped the slimy, grotesque head inside.

Paris, the Bonnie to his Clyde, opened the garage of the condo, pulling her car all the way in, parking it next to Kenya's. When the door was shut and the coast was clear, London, Paris, and O.T. struggled to drag the freakishly heavy body out. On the count of three, they lifted Deacon, throwing him into the trunk. The weight caused the new car to bounce downwards to the garage pavement before slowly lifting back up. O.T. made the comment they should've driven his truck. Both Paris and London gave him the "as if you knew you were coming to remove a dead body, nigga, tonight" side eye.

"O.T., baby we need to get cleaned up and at least get this blood off of our clothes," Paris, thinking well ahead, suggested. "We don't want to get pulled over in this neighborhood with these clothes on."

"I've got nine motherfucking reasons none of these white Rodney King–ass-beating sons of bitches betta not fuck with nan one of us tonight!" O.T. raised his shirt up, revealing his pistol as well as his washboard abs that he spent hours working out to achieve. "But you right, I'm gonna go back upstairs and get some of Storm's gear to throw on. I'll grab one of Kenya's track suits for you."

"Thanks, boo." Paris leaned over, giving him a fast kiss on the lips. "Hurry up, okay? I don't want Deacon's blood and the rest of those fluids to leak through that blanket and stain the trunk carpet. You know how much they be charging to detail shit like that out!"

London stood back, amazed at the calm and coolness of the couple. It was as if they encountered this type of bizarre occurrence on a daily basis. *What has Kenya gotten me into? This is pure madness!* She pondered silently, wishing she was anywhere in the world other than where she was, doing what she was doing. *One day I'm at school, working toward my degree; the next, I'm tangled up in covering up not one, but two murders. God, this is so messed up—so wrong!*

After washing their faces and hands, getting themselves looking somewhat halfway decent, O.T. and Paris were ready to roll. With Paris behind the wheel, they cautiously drove off, trying to look as inconspicuous as possible. This was the one time, if any, that the gangsta love duo didn't need to get pulled over by the cops.

The two of them would dispose of the body, while O.T. left his new partner in crime, London, in charge of getting Kenya's panicked, grief-stricken-ass together. Maybe London could get her sister to postpone her sudden hysterical breakdown and relax so that they could figure this strange mystery out.

Now was definitely not the time for any of the three to punk out and fold. If ever there was a night that a person had to think and react with their mind and not their heart, this, hands-down, would be that goddamned night.

5

It Just Got Real

Kenya was all cried out. Full of emotion, she walked down the stairs to find her sister trying her best to salvage whatever she could from the lower level of the home. "Hey, sis," Kenya sniffed, pushing the redial button on her phone. "Is O.T. back yet? Have you seen him or Paris?"

"Oh, please, stop it! Don't you think you would have heard that loud, obnoxious Negro you deal with?" London barked, going from room to room, throwing stuff into a garbage bag.

"Girl, he's not that bad, girl!" For the first time since they had returned from the airport, Kenya gave her twin a slight grin, holding the phone to her ear. "You just gotta get used to him. He'll grow on you after a while."

"Well, I'm sorry. I have no intentions whatsoever of him growing on me. I feel sorry for his girlfriend and anyone else that has the misfortune to spend any more than ten minutes in his presence." London went on making wise comments pertaining to O.T.'s offbeat character. "He's a real jerk if I ever met one! She's a better woman than me."

Kenya held up her hand to shush London while she tried to leave another message in Storm's voice mail. However, it already was full, making that task impossible. Kenya was heated all over again, throwing her phone against the still-wet walls. Pounding her fist on the table, worry started once more to consume her thoughts. London, startled, ran from the kitchen to see her sister enraged.

"I swear to God I'm gonna kill a motherfucker if something done happened to him! I swear I am—I swear!"

"Calm down, Kenya!" London urged.

Just as Kenya finished ranting, Paris and O.T. returned. London wasted no time in opening the door to let the pair inside.

"Did you find out something?" Kenya rushed up to O.T., almost knocking him off his feet. "Did he call? Have you heard anything? Tell me he called you!"

"Naw, baby girl," he regretfully hated to say. "But I did find out that fugazy wannabe playa Royce's new number and shit."

"Well, was he with them? Do he know something? Where did he say Storm was?"

"Kenya, pump ya brakes, will ya?" O.T. said, moving her to the side so that Paris could get all the way in the condo door. "His phone goes straight to voice mail too. I tried calling that fool at least a good ten times—same thing—voice mail."

"Damn!" Kenya shook her head, desperate for any information to ease her fears.

"Relax, girl!" Paris spoke up, hugging her friend. "It's gonna be okay. Storm is a soldier—you know that. He's gonna call. Don't worry—you'll see."

"When I get you and your sister settled, I'm gonna shoot by Royce's peoples and try to find out if they heard from him yet. Just try to chill," he reasoned, obviously still worried himself. "I'm on it!"

"I'm trying to be calm, but this whole thing don't make no sense to me at all!" Kenya whimpered, not being able to hold back another round of tears. "I need to stay here just in case he come home!"

"Listen up, girl. Me and Paris done handled the Deacon situation for now, may he rest in peace, but I still don't think it's safe in here. Whoever did all this and killed my manz might come back. Y'all should just jet until we hear something."

"No damn kidding, Sherlock," London interrupted, ready to be anywhere but there.

The tension in the air and dislike she was feeling for O.T. was transparent and obvious to the entire room. Being a career class-A asshole was second nature to O.T., so he was used to people having an instant hatred of him. Brushing her smart comments off as nothing, he finished his statement without even missing a beat.

"Look, I'll fall through tomorrow myself and really clean up the bathroom and that nasty-ass fish tank with bleach and some of that strong-ass industrial-strength disinfectant that's down at the club. We can't risk letting anybody else inside here until we know what's what."

Everyone, even Kenya, agreed with O.T. that it would be for the best for the twins to vacate the premises, at least for the time being. Paris, loyal to the end, started to help London gather some of Kenya's things, so she and O.T. could take them to get a hotel room until they could get a handle on the real deal and sometime down the line get some workmen over to survey and repair the damaged condo. Besides, it was no way on God's green earth that the girls were gonna feel comfortable spending one night in a spot where who-knows-what had taken place.

***

"Come on, y'all got enough stuff for a few days."

"All right, O.T., we're coming." Kenya replied. After close to a hour of being in the house, all four of them emerged out onto the small porch. O.T. carried most of the bags to Kenya's car, while Paris grabbed the rest. London stood over toward the far side of the door as Kenya locked up, trying to secure the rest of her belongings even though crime almost never occurred in their secure community. In the midst of all the commotion that'd taken place since their arrival from Detroit, the overflowing of the flower-design mailbox was overlooked.

"Hey, Kenya, it looks as if you've got a lot of mail piled up in this box. You want me to get it?"

"Yeah, London—grab it out for me. Just throw all that mess in your bag. It ain't probably shit but a bunch of bills and catalogues. I ain't got time to give a damn about that junk now!"

Kenya double-checked the locks on the condo door; the same locks that failed to keep the intruders out. London stuffed all the mail, including a small-sized manila envelope, in her purse without even a second thought. She didn't take notice that a small parcel had nothing written on it front or back; meaning that more than likely, someone had to have left it in the mailbox personally.

***

After both taking showers, trying to unpack a few things and relax, Kenya laid across the bed dialing Storm's number once more, while London emptied the items in her purse onto the dresser in search of a comb and a brush.

"Oh snap! What was that?" Startled, she leaped backwards, almost tripping over her own feet.

"What's wrong, London? What is it?"

"Girl, there's something moving in this envelope."

"What envelope?"

"That one—right there," London pointed from afar.

"You bugging! Where did you get it from? And what you mean *moving*?"

"Stop playing with me, fool! It's the mail from your house, Kenya! That's where I got it from!"

"Well, who is it addressed to?" Kenya bit her lower lip as they both moved over closer toward the hotel door.

Bzzzzzzzz . . . The envelope vibrated once again.

"Go over there, London, and see what it is."

"Excuse me, Miss Kenya, but that's your dang-gone package, not mine! It came from your house—your mail! So you go!"

"Okay, but come with me," Kenya bargained with her sister.

As they slowly approached the dresser, the mystery mail buzzed once more. Kenya bravely reached over, carefully picking the package up with two fingers. Moving slowly, she walked over to the lamp on the desk. Taking a deep breath, she tried holding it up to the light, but couldn't make out its contents.

"Just open it," London insisted, knowing if it was a fragile bomb they'd both be dead by now. "It's not explosive, but be careful of poison."

"Okay, okay, okay!" Kenya tore open the envelope, dumping what was inside onto the bed.

"I'm confused. A silly old cell phone and an old burgundy-velvet ring box?" London casually asked, expecting something more. "Who would send you stuff like that?"

Kenya placed her hand over her mouth to muffle her scream. "That's Storm's cell phone! He's the only one who I know that has a neon-green antenna on his shit and an airbrushed tiger on the back! That's his phone!"

"Are you sure?"

"Yeah, London, I'm certain. This is definitely his!" Kenya snatched the phone off the bed, flipping it open. It said the words *Capacity Full* across the screen.

"What about the ring box, Kenya? Have you seen it before or what? What's in it?" the twin asked her confused sister.

"I'm still bugging out on this phone," Kenya told her sibling, holding it up in her hand.

"Well, I'm gonna open it." London leaned over, swooping up the small velvet box, shaking it slightly before peeking inside.

"What's in there?" Kenya waited before starting to go through Storm's phone for any clues to his whereabouts.

"Oh, my God! Ugh!" London dropped the box on the carpet, revealing a small note and what appeared to be a severed piece of an earlobe with a diamond earring still attached. To Kenya's dismay, it was the same earring that Deacon was wearing; the same one that she also owned. It was Storm's. It had to be. Now it was proof positive that Storm was definitely injured badly, in danger or worse than that, dead.

Kenya, exhausted from grief, fell to the carpet, passing out. As her twin sister lay sprawled out on the hotel-room floor, London didn't know what else to do. Without hesitation, she rushed to the telephone, dialing the number that O.T. left for her. There was no need calling the cops for assistance. The way Kenya, Paris, and O.T. made it seem, they couldn't help anyhow.

6

You Owe Me!

O.T. found the girls scrunched together down in the corner, near the door of the hotel room. "Where is it at?" He scanned the room with his eyes darting around.

"By the side of the bed." Kenya threw her hand in the direction of the small box. "It's over there."

O.T. swiftly bolted to the other side of the bed, bending down on one knee. London watched the cocky, perfect muscle-ripped, sagged-jeans, baseball-cap-backwards–wearing thug, turn into melted butter as he held the evidence of his brother's apparent harm in his rough, seemingly strong hands. London could now for the first time since encountering O.T. somehow relate to his pain. Just like that, he now was a human in her eyes, instead of a beast, as he let his guard down, sobbing loudly.

"Please don't cry. We're gonna figure something out. I promise." London cradled him in her arms while her sister escaped to throw up in the bathroom. She had been in Dallas less than twenty-four hours and was already entangled in obstruction of justice and another murder. Including Swift, the hit man back home, that was two altogether.

"I'm tight, uhm . . . London." O.T. could barely remember her name with all the chaos that was going on that night. He wanted to call her Kenya, but he caught himself. He stood up first, reaching his hand downwards to assist London to her feet. As they were standing face-to-face, O.T. leaned in close, moving London's hair out of her eyes. Her inexperienced romantic heart was working overtime. She shut her eyes and waited for him to kiss her. Feeling his body get closer, she held her breath in anticipation.

"Listen, London," he whispered in her ear. "We good, right? You ain't gonna tell nobody about that little punk-ass-faggot crying bullshit, are you? A guy slipped up on that female tip."

"What?" London was pissed, to say the least and disappointed that all O.T. was ultimately worried about was people knowing that he was normal and had normal reactions to abnormal circumstances. Her sudden compassion and fascination with him had come to a quick halt. "Is that all you concerned with—what people think?"

"Naw, but . . ."

Kenya came back into the room on the tail end of the conversation between them. "What's going on in here?"

"Nothing, Kenya," O.T. answered for both.

"Yeah, nothing!" London happily agreed.

You owe me and a phone number was written on the note that was stuffed inside the box.

"What does that mean?" Kenya rubbed both sweaty hands together. "*You owe me*? Owe who? Owe what?"

"We gotta call this number and hopefully we can find out." O.T. pulled out his cell phone, dialing the mystery person. After a few rings, what had to be an older-sounding man answered his call. Listening attentively, it was a voice that wasn't familiar to O.T. at all.

"Yeah!" the guy repeated twice before he got a response from Storm's brother. "I hope you're ready to listen? And pay attention!"

"This O.T., who this?" he finally blurted out, wanting some answers.

"Listen, let me make this perfectly clear, I'm asking the questions here, young man, not you. Is that understood?"

"Who the fuck is this?" O.T. was losing his patience with the man at the other end of the line.

"Tsk, tsk. Now, is that any way to address your elders?" The man also was growing seemingly frustrated of all the cat-and-mouse talk. "Didn't your project-living, three-part-time-job-working, two-different-baby-daddy having, now-crackhead mother teach you or your brother any manners?"

"Huh, what did you just say?" O.T. was thrown off his square as the girls looked on.

"You heard perfectly well what I just said and believe me, I'm not in the mood or accustomed to repetitious conversation!"

"Yo nigga, how you know shit about my ol' girl?"

"Trust me. I know everything about your entire family. From your sorry excuse for a father, your brother murdered, to your third cousin twice removed on your mother's side—and by the way, I don't like to use the term *nigga*! I find it derogatory and barbaric."

O.T. was completely outraged by the stranger's overly blatant disrespect for him and his family. "Listen, dude! Where the fuck is my brother at? I swear to God, if you—"

The man cut him off, laughing. "You swear to God what? I'm not amused. Please refrain from making idle threats you can't possibly back up. I have come in the past not to appreciate them nor tolerate them. So now, if you don't mind, can we get to the business at hand, youngster, your brother's life or what's left of it."

O.T. was, for the first time since the call was placed, silent. He looked at Kenya and London, both sitting on the edge of the bed, anxiously waiting to hear any news.

The man started with the answer to O.T.'s original question. "This is Javier and your brother, Storm, is here with me. For the time being he is safe from harm's way. And trust, if all goes as planned, he will stay that way. You have my word on that much, but the outcome depends on you."

"How can he be safe, you lunatic?" O.T. grew more enraged staring at the ring box. "Ain't this a chunk of his damn ear and shit? You a sick-ass bastard for doing this!"

"What did I just mention about your mouth, young man? Any further outburst and name-calling will cause me to bring this call to an abrupt end—terminated. Are we clear?"

"Yeah, we clear." A once-again silent O.T. sat still after being scolded like a child.

"Now, as I was saying. Storm is here with me and alive, for the time being. If you have possession of this number, it is very safe to assume that you already have come in contact with your brother's business partner and associate, Deacon. Is this much true?"

"Yeah, if that's what you wanna call it." O.T. was being sarcastic and bitter. "Man, that shit was foul as hell! How could y'all do some old crazy stuff like that?"

"That's life in the game we all chose to play—you, me, your brother, and the recently departed Deacon. Now deal with it!" Javier chuckled before revealing some truths. "Your brother and his twisted personal life, has caused me and my various operations throughout the region major financial strains that must be satisfied."

"How so? I know for a fact he has never been short on a single payment to anyone on any package."

"Well, because of him, his ex-stripper girlfriend, and her do-good sister, I just have been made aware of my cash flow has been slowing down and that is not acceptable—not acceptable at all."

O.T. looked at the girls and felt a deep veil of hatred come over him. He now knew that it was because of them that his big brother was in serious trouble as he spoke. "What's the deal, old man? What you want?" O.T. wanted to skip straight to the point of their conversation. He wanted to know exactly what it would take to get Storm back safe and sound.

"Well, it seems London Roberts, his soon-to-be sister-in-law and her little group P.A.I.D., have been causing a few bumps in the road here and there," Javier spoke calmly in an even tone. "There was some confusion as to the identity of her and her twin Kenya, the dancer whore, at first, but that mystery has since been solved. A recently ex-employee of mine, a one Mr. Swift, ill-fatedly found out the hard way, but as the game goes it's always casualty in war."

"What?" O.T. asked, confused.

"So goes life," Javier coldly remarked.

"What the hell is P.A.I.D.? And who is Swift?" O.T. inquired, as he attentively kept his ear pressed to the telephone receiver. "I don't follow you! What the fuck does any of that bullshit mean?"

"Listen, O.T., you have to ask your peoples any questions you need answers to. They can fill you in on their part in all this. My main concern right now is my revenue and nothing more. By my calculations, your brother Storm owes me approximately two hundred and fifty thousand dollars in lost sales. Although it's true he never has been late on his own payments, he is being held responsible for his peoples' actions, as it may."

"Two hundred and fifty thousand dollars! Are you nuts? That shit just ain't right, dude. What fucking people? What you mean?"

"Well, I guess that Storm's safe return doesn't mean that much to you." Javier still remained calm. "I'm sorry to have troubled you. I guess that this is good-bye and have a good life!"

"No, no! Wait!" O.T. stuttered, wasting no time reconsidering. "I'll get the money, I'll get it! But it's gonna take me some time. That's a helluva lot of bread to come up with just like that!"

"I'm aware of that and no one can say I'm not a fair man, so I will give you at least—shall we say—thirty days to gather it. Are we clear on the time frame or what?"

"Yeah, we clear. I'll call you as soon as I get the cash together. I swear to God I'ma get it, but how do I know Storm is even still alive?"

"You don't—not for sure. It's a gamble you have to take. And by the way, there's no need in calling this number again. I'll get back in touch with you when necessary," he vehemently demanded. "Thirty days youngster, no more."

And with that exchange Javier hung the phone up, leaving O.T. to explain to Kenya and London what was needed, not to mention get some of his own questions answered.

"What did they say? Where is Storm? Is he hurt bad? Is he coming home?" Kenya fired question after question. "Please tell me what whoever was on the phone said—please!"

"Well, bottom line is, thanks to you and this bitch right here, we supposedly owe Javier two hundred and fifty thousand Gs to get Storm back home. If we pay the dough, the old man claim he'll let him go fucking free." O.T. was pissed and made no excuses as he mean-mugged London for being the direct cause for the financial uphill battle he was now facing.

"What do you mean, two hundred and fifty thousand dollars?" Kenya was left puzzled by O.T.'s comments. "And why the fuck you calling my sister a bitch? What she got to do with Storm or Deacon?"

"What the hell is P.A.I.D.?" he fumed, slamming his fist down on the nightstand, causing it to tilt over. "Can one of y'all identical bookends tell me that?"

London and Kenya quickly made eye contact with one another. It was now painfully apparent that Storm's sudden disappearance and Deacon's murder were all linked back to London's one true passion, People Against Illegal Drugs. The connection was all coming together.

"Damn frick and frack! Is one of y'all hoes gonna answer my damn question? Don't speak at one time! What is P.A.I.D.?" O.T. was now on his feet, towering over the girls. "And who is this dead nigga, Swift? Y'all need to start talking quick!"

Kenya jumped up in his face. "Hold the hell on, motherfucker. Me or my sister ain't gonna be anymore bitches or hoes, that's first of all. We can get that straight off rip!"

"What you just say?" O.T. spit out wildly, also caught in his emotions. "What you say?"

"You heard me, black man. I'm gonna explain everything and shit, but you not just about to come up here in our room and dog us the hell out. That ain't flying!"

"Oh, yeah! Is that right?" His nostrils flared and the veins in his neck were ready to burst.

"Yeah, it's right, O.T." Kenya suddenly pounced up and swung on him. "I know shit is real messed up right about now and we all upset and worried about Storm, but you got me all fucked up! You better act like you know, nigga!" With all her big talk, her punch missed its mark.

O.T. admired Kenya's off-the-wall crazy spunk and backed down to hear her explain. "All right then." He casually sat back in one of the chairs, folding his arms. "I'm listening and please don't leave shit out."

"I ain't!"

"Good! Then speak!"

London was preparing herself for all the fireworks that were sure to jump. She knew that she was gonna be number one on O.T.'s shit list, but so be it.

"Well, first off, P.A.I.D. is an organization that my sister, London, and her roommate Fatima started back east in college."

"And?" O.T. was growing impatient. "Go on!"

"Damn! Calm down and let me finish."

"Go ahead, Kenya. I said I'm listening!"

"Like I was saying . . ." She rolled her eyes, clearing her throat. "My sister and her roommate were up at school and got together with a few other students to form a kids-against-drugs sort of a club."

London jumped in the conversation, clarifying what exactly it was. "It's called People Against Illegal Drugs, and FYI, it is more than just a small handful of my classmates, it's almost the entire campus of my university, as well as several other schools." She had her chest stuck out as she bragged about the strength of the group, not yet realizing the group was the reason behind the kidnapping and murder.

"Can you please shut the fuck up, London? Is you trying to make shit worse or what?" Kenya had to put her twin in her place. Even though London was busy trying to act all high and mighty, real talk, it was her bullshit that had Storm being held hostage and Kenya knew it.

"Yeah, London! Shut the fuck up!" O.T. co-signed with Kenya as he waved her off with his hand in a dismissive fashion.

London did as she was told and let her sister finish speaking, but gave O.T. the finger.

"Anyhow, the organization kinda spread out here to the South, I guess. I'm sure that's the group that Storm and Deacon were complaining about the other day. You know what I'm talking about, don't you?"

O.T. was disgusted as he stared at London. "You mean to tell me that all along your damn sister has been fucking shit up for our pockets?"

Kenya hated to admit to him that he was right, so she turned her back on him as she continued to explain. "I didn't put two and two together until a few minutes ago my damn self." She glanced over at London while running her fingers through her tangled hair.

"Okay, then. What about this buster named Swift? What's his role in all of this? Is that your ho-ass man?" O.T. directed his assault of questions to London.

"No, he's the man who tried to kill us!" she shouted out loudly for the whole world to hear. "In our own home, Mr. Know So Much. He tried to kill us! And right about now, I would rather be back in Detroit and take my chances with another lunatic murderer than be in this godforsaken town with you!" She sneered with contempt. "He was probably one of your dope-dealing cohorts anyway!"

London's boisterous outburst left O.T. and Kenya dumbfounded. It was the most words that O.T. heard come out her mouth all evening.

"Bitch, is you crazy? Who the fuck is you call yourself talking to?"

"Come on, y'all. We need to put all this petty junk on the back burner 'til we pony up on that loot and get Storm back." Kenya brought an immediate end to the heated exchange as she looked over at the small ring box and the tiny chunk of severed earlobe. "It don't matter what the fuck happened, the main agenda is Storm. The hell with that dumb shit, y'all two can fight it out later if you want. We ain't got time to waste. We need to see how much money we already have toward the two hundred and fifty Gs so we can get my man back home."

Kenya took a pen out her purse and grabbed the hotel stationery out the desk drawer. Calculating the ticket money from the workers in the streets, including the dope that they had stashed in reserves and the dough that Kenya had retrieved from the house floor safe, they were still very much short of their needed goal.

Much to London and O.T.'s surprise, Kenya announced that she was holding close to a little over a hundred grand in cash. She also made it clear that when she went to the bank to her

safe deposit box, she planned on pawning the
jewelry that Storm always insisted that she kept
there. Lumped together with the cash O.T. had
from Alley Cats, they still came up 135,000 dollars short. They had to devise a scheme to come
up on the balance.

Kenya gave her twin a dirty look. She had
only, just several months earlier, given London
15,000 dollars out the kindness of her heart,
that she knew good and damn well that London
was still holding on to that and all her other
savings, for that matter. Here now, her identical
twin sister sat on the edge of the bed, quiet
as a church mouse, not even speaking up and
volunteering to give the cash she was blessed
with back to help free Storm and bring him
safely home. From that moment on, Kenya
knew things would never be the same between
the two.

In a last-ditch attempt for London to jump in
and have her sister's back, she spoke out softly
in fear of the response, if any. "I also got some
money coming in a week or so from the sale of
my grandmother's house back in Detroit that I
can kick in," Kenya said, sighing.

London still remained hush-mouthed, not
offering her share of Gran's house, breaking
Kenya's heart.

O.T. wrapped his arms around Kenya, who he could see had a game plan immediately in the works. "Don't worry. A nigga like me got a few more irons burning in the fire. We'll get it all by thirty days!" he reassuringly whispered in her ear. "I ain't gonna just let my brother's life go just like that if I can stop it!"

London watched the exchange of embraces from the two of them and felt strangely jealous for some odd reason. *Kenya gets every cute guy she wants.* She wanted to run across the room and rip her promiscuously rumored sister out O.T.'s arms and take her place. As the girls looked each other in the eye, London got a cold vibe from her sister. She knew Kenya like the back of her hand and knew that her twin wanted her to give up her share of the revenue from the sale of the house and give the money back she'd given her—just because. Without a second thought, there was no way in sweet fire hell that she was throwing her inheritance out the window on some lowlife drug dealer who she never had even met. *How could she put me in that position to risk losing my tuition money? What nerve! I see she still hasn't changed!*

7

Da Grind

The days that soon followed were consumed with argument after argument between the twins. Each one of them was on edge for obvious different reasons. London missed being back on campus with all of her friends, trying to achieve her degree, while Kenya focused her entire mental and physical strength on getting her drug-dealer fiancé back home in one piece. London knew that her sister had an attitude with her about her reluctance to contribute revenue to the Save Storm Fund, but so damn what.

"How long are you going to stump around this room and not speak to me?" London finally inquired. "You need to grow up and handle things more maturely. I mean, none of this makes any sense."

"Excuse the hell outta me! Some of us can't go through bullshit and just blow it off like you. Everyone is not as frigid as you are!" Kenya cut her eyes, rolling them to the top of her head. "I'm trying to get this loot together to get my boo home, not that you give a damn! He's the most important thing in my life! Do you understand that?"

After clearing her throat, London fired back her own round of profound words. "Look, I truly care about you, not him. You best believe, if it was you that needed my money or my help, I would be right there, jimmy on the spot. Haven't I proved that to you time after time?" At this point she was all up in Kenya's grill, not giving her an inch to move. "If my memory serves me correct, wasn't I the one who just helped your funny-acting so-called friends carry a corpse to the car while you were busy putting on one of your all-too-famous drama queen roles? That was me doing all that!"

Kenya couldn't understand why her sister was being so callous and coldhearted, but didn't have the time to figure it out. It was only one thing on her mind, Storm. Keeping her eye on the prize, she finished getting dressed and left a disrespectful London in the hotel room to fuss, argue, and be judgmental by herself. O.T. had called earlier and wanted Kenya to meet him down at the club, so she assumed he had an update that he didn't want to share over the phone.

When Kenya drove up to the club, she pulled into her parking space. As she stepped out the cool, air-conditioned truck and into the sweltering Dallas heat, Kenya looked over to the empty space next to hers, also labeled RESERVED. *Don't worry baby. I'm gonna bring ya ass home where you belong*, she thought as she got the door keys to Alley Cats out of her purse and cautiously approached the entrance. Before she got a chance to unlock all the security doors, O.T. skirted up in the lot doing at least 80 mph. He had the music blasting as usual; straight foolin'. Kenya, on edge, was spooked by him burning rubber and almost took a shit in her panties.

"What's wrong with your crazy-ass, fool?" were the first words that flew out her mouth when he got out his pimped-out ride.

O.T. ran over to a visibly heated Kenya, picking her up off her feet and swinging her around. "I got some good news for you—real fucking good!"

"What is it? What is it?" She smiled, temporarily forgetting about his well-known idiotic actions. "Did you talk to Storm? Is he okay? Hurry up and tell me!"

"Naw Kenya, I haven't heard from him." He put her down, seeing she was getting the wrong impression of his news. "But I got us some more loot to throw in the pot, plus a line on a good-ass hustle that might push us over the top on that ho-ass buster, Javier's ticket."

Kenya was noticeably disappointed that O.T. hadn't gotten any more news about his brother; yet coming up with some more money would ease the load.

They both entered the club after disarming the alarm and got down to business. He informed Kenya that he was gonna set up a meeting in the club on Friday evening. He explained that he could double up on some good dope that he'd gotten a line on and possibly make all the money they needed. Encouraged, Kenya took her notebook out so that they could add up the new figures.

O.T. eagerly took 35,000 dollars cash out a shoe box that was behind the bar on the shelf and tossed it to Kenya. "Here you go. Add this."

Kenya reached for the stacks of currency that were crispy and smelled new. "Where did you get this from?" She was leery as she took another whiff, inspecting the bank-issued bands. "I hope your behind didn't do what I think you did! Please tell me you didn't!"

"Dig this here. Don't be so damn quick to always think the worse about me." He paused as he checked his brother's woman and opened up a beer. After two long gulps, he finally eased Kenya's mind, answering her question. "Your girl Paris done emptied out her bank account and pawned some of her jewelry. You know she's down on my team and yours and Storm's! You know she got your back!"

Kenya sat back on the bar stool, letting out a long, drawn-out sigh of built-up denial. She couldn't believe that her best friend Paris would kick in all her life savings and risk losing her jewelry, while her own flesh-and-blood twin sister couldn't care less. "Paris always is there when I need her. You better treat her right, boy! She deserves that!" Kenya pointed her finger at O.T., trying extra-hard to reinforce her words. "I ain't playing with you either, Negro. You need to make it legal like me and Storm is gonna do as soon as he gets home—get married and stop running these streets."

O.T. guzzled down the rest of the beer in the bottle and twisted the top off another. "Please Kenya, you know I'm a damn pimp!" He yanked at his manhood and chuckled loudly. "Matter of fact, where is that fat-ass big-mouth twin sister of yours at? Why she ain't roll with you down here? I got something for her!"

Kenya got up from the bar stool, stuffing the money in her purse. With her keys in her hand, heading toward the door, she laughed at his remarks. "Okay playa playa. You best to stick with Paris. She's the only one who will put up with your foul, crab-ass behavior you be dishing out. And as for London, I think—naw, let me rephrase that bullshit—I know that she is a little bit out your reach, son. So you need to push on off that thought. My sister don't even get down like that, homeboy, so beat it!"

"Oh, yeah—okay? We'll see!" O.T. gave Kenya the side eye from across the club.

Kenya was pissed with London for being so cheap, but that still didn't stop her from chin-checking O.T. on his always reckless behavior. "Dude, go home to your woman with your ignorant ass and I'll see you Friday!"

O.T. was left standing in the club alone. Looking around, he started reminiscing about him, Deacon, and Storm playing pool and talking shit. O.T., feeling depressed, poured himself a double shot of yak, agonizing what the near future would bring. He knew that sooner or later he would have to end up making up some sort of a lie to Deacon's only family member who he knew of. It was only a matter of time before that he's-on-a-vacation bullshit would play out. How would he or anyone for that matter, explain to Deacon's churchgoing, Bible-toting grandma that her only grandson was kidnapped and murdered, gruesomely beheaded, no less.

The rest of the afternoon well off into the evening, O.T. sat in the back booth of the empty, dark, deserted club getting pissy drunk, smoking blunts. His thoughts were consumed with thinking about Deacon's decapitated body that he and Paris buried in a shallow grave in the back of an old, abandoned warehouse and, of course, getting up on the rest of the money he needed to get his brother home safely. Like the true dog he was, once or twice in the evening he even found the time to think about running up in Kenya's twin sister as a worried Paris blew up his cell phone, praying he was okay.

8

How Dare You

It was early Friday evening and Alley Cats was turned up on total bump. Everyone had come out for the club's most popular night, freak-out Fridays, which meant a lobster, crab, and shrimp buffet dinner along with a bottle of Moët with each time a customer got three dances or more from a girl in the VIP room. They always had a couple more bouncers on duty on the weekends for all the extra crowd that would pack in. Paris and Kenya were out shopping one day and came up with the idea as a promotional gimmick to ensure they got the guys to stop in the club and spend a portion of their weekly paychecks with them before they took the rest home to their nagging wives and pesky kids.

O.T. was busy posted behind the bar, giving one of his constant power-drunk speeches to Dawson, the head bartender, on watering down the drinks in order to save a few dollars. Even though he knew that Storm or Deacon didn't believe in shortchanging the customers on drinks, dances, or dinner, he let their absence go to his head. Paris, a team player, was occupied with collecting the house fee from the dancers before they stepped on stage and made their rounds of hustling the guys for tips. Staying on top of the girls was always Kenya's job, but she was running late, causing Paris to fill in for her.

With the clipboard in hand she checked off the names as they paid. Passion, Too Sweet, Addiction, Butter, Fatal Beauty, Tight-n-Right, Temptation, Sugar, Li'l Bit, Lexus, Phat Cat, and lastly Chocolate Bunny's nasty, big booty, trifling, always on the verge of getting fired for breaking the club rules, had all taken care of their business and were already on the grind, roaming the floor and getting that money.

"Will you hurry up, London? I've gotta get down to the club. We already late as a fuck and plus it's Friday night, so speed that ass up!" Kenya knocked at the bathroom door three times in an attempt to get her sister to rush things along. "Now come on and stop all that bullshitting around! We gotta bounce unless you staying here! The choice is yours!"

London was usually the one who was on time, but this was somewhat a special occasion for her. She was gonna come face-to-face with O.T. for the first time since that horrible night they met. London, for some strange reason, couldn't take her mind off of him. She kept Kenya up the night before asking question after question about his rude demeanor and if he was serious about Paris. Even though London tried her best playing it off, her twin was vibin' with her and could see right through her game. Kenya didn't have to twist London's arm one bit into going to work with her at the strip club she always said was so degrading to women. Especially when she found out O.T. was gonna be on the premises.

Paris was Kenya's best friend and it was no way on God's green earth that she was going to be a part of causing her even a moment's worth of pain. Blood ain't always thicker than water, and in this case it couldn't be truer. So if that meant cock-blocking her sister, then so be it. It would be done. After ten more minutes past by, London exited the bathroom with a brand-new bounce in her step and a huge grin plastered on her face.

"I don't know what in the fuck your slick-ass is so slap-happy about. Storm is still out there somewhere hurt and you all *hee-hee-ha-ha-ing*,"

Kenya agitatedly announced. "You act like you don't even care! Girl, let's go so I can make this money!"

"What?"

"You heard me! Stop smiling and let's go!"

"What, so it's against the law now to smile in Dallas until your drug-dealing boyfriend comes home?" London returned her sister's sarcasm, giving as good as she got. "Well, excuse me for living!"

"Listen here, Ms. Thang! While you being so smarted-mouthed and in the mirror primping, in case you have overlooked one damn thing, well, let me remind you, O.T. already has a wifey—Paris—remember her?" Kenya placed both hands on her hips and bucked her eyes. "So if you have any designs on him in any form or fashion, you better forget about it, college girl, and keep that shit straight moving. We clear? Understand?"

"Whatever, Kenya! I don't know what you're talking about. I don't like that lowlife, rude thug. That's more your style."

"Yeah, right! Whatever, my ass! Just don't forget what I just said." Kenya pushed London's arm. "He got a girl—my best friend!"

After the exchange the twin sisters finally left the hotel en route to Alley Cats, where it was destined to be one helluva long night.

***

"Hey, Kenya, how are—" With the twins standing before him, Boz, the head of security, couldn't believe what he was seeing, having the exact same reaction as O.T. and Paris.

"Close your mouth, Boz, before something flies in it."

"But—" He was stunned.

"I know, silly. This is my twin sister, London. Do me a favor and let her in the office through the back door—and oh, please don't mention her being here to anyone. Not to the other bouncers, the dancers, or anybody else on the staff. Okay?"

Boz's eyes were glued to London as he walked with her around to the rear of the club. He noticed that although she was indeed a mirror image of Kenya's face, their mannerisms were outrageously miles different. Kenya walked like a panther, seductively on the prowl for the weak, while London took each step with pride and confidence, head held high with an air of arrogance.

London, perceptive of her surroundings in light of recent events, glanced over, detecting his strange, silly expression. "Is there something wrong? Do I have a glob of snot hanging from my nose or what?" She winked, knowing he was another person in Kenya's life who failed to know about her existence.

"Oh, my bad. I didn't know the boss's girl had a twin, that's all." Boz laughed it off, showing his mouthful of gold-plated teeth. "It ain't no problem. It's just bugged out, that's all."

Going inside the strip club's doors and up the rear stairs, London caught a brief glance at the neon-lit stage. One of the dancers was hanging upside down from the brass pole, while others were sitting backwards in men's laps grinding, simulating sexual acts. When settled down on the couch in the plush office, her mind began to wonder and she felt saddened. London realized that only a short time ago, her sister Kenya was one of these low-self-esteemed females.

"Hey, Paris. Sorry I'm late. How are things going so far? All these hoes out here paid?" Kenya found her friend in the dressing room going over some of the house rules for a new dancer named Jordan, who grew up around the way from Paris.

"Hey, woman! I was just thinking about where the heck your crazy-ass was at."

"Girl, you know I'm traveling with a little extra baggage these days," Kenya replied low-key, referring to her sister.

"Oh yeah, Kenya, dig that."

"So, how things going in here so far? How we looking?"

Paris finished up schooling the new dancer on the dos and don'ts of the club and went into the hallway, followed by Kenya. "Everything's everything. We got a full house already and it isn't even eight yet. I already went in the kitchen and told them to get some more food prepped."

"That's what's up!" Kenya nodded, feeling positive. "We need all the cheddar that we can scramble up on. We definitely getting closer—especially thanks to you!"

Paris gave her girl a hug that was cut short by one of the dancers, Chocolate Bunny, who was walking fast, yelling out to one of the bouncers. Her manner was louder and much more ghetto than normal. It was obvious by the way she was waving her hands around and bopping from side to side like her neck was broke, someone had gotten on her bad side, which was almost 100 percent impossible to do, since Chocolate Bunny had an anything-goes policy, aka, "Fuck you—pay me."

"Excuse me, Paris. Let me see what in the hell is going on with that dirty-black skank headed this way. You know she always got some drama stirring!"

Paris was glad that Kenya was finally there to intervene. If it was one female in the entire club that she despised, it was Chocolate Bunny. It was no secret to Paris or any other person that worked in Alley Cats that O.T. had fucked around with her back in the day. And still, every chance that Chocolate Bunny got to get close to O.T., she took advantage, at times rubbing their past "special friendship" in Paris's face.

Paris, a nutcase and street soldier in her own right, wanted to kick her black-ass on several occasions and had to be physically held back by some of the other dancers and a bartender. Feeling some sort of way, she often lobbied for Storm or Deacon to fire Chocolate Bunny's slimeball behind on the spot for her disrespectful antics, but she was one of Alley Cats's main attractions and made a lot of dough for the club. That meant that Paris had to suck it up for the cause, like it or leave it and be a big girl.

"What's the deal? What's wrong?" Pretending to be sympathetic, Kenya placed her hand on the drama-prone dancer's sweaty shoulder. "Calm down and tell me! What's going on?"

"Hey, Kenya!" Chocolate Bunny looked at her with blood in her eyes. "It's that old-ass wannabe pimp that y'all had us chillin' with before. Well, he must be nuts and got me messed all the way up!"

"Nicole, slow down. Who are you talking about?"

"Are you fucking crazy, Kenya! Don't be using my motherfucking government name in this bitch!"

If it had been any other circumstance that went down and a dancer, especially Chocolate Bunny, had screamed on Kenya like that, moneymaker or not, the bitch would hit the bricks, bottom line. Yet Kenya knew better than to use someone's real name in the club if they weren't into broadcasting it themselves. A lot of perverts and stalkers sat around nursing their drinks in hopes of finding out where some of the girls of their dreams lived at and getting a dancer's legal name would be that gateway. Kenya didn't mind taking a cop this one instance, because she would've felt the same way if someone did it to her back at Heads Up.

"Damn girl, I'm sorry. It slipped." Kenya wasn't fronting, she truly was. "I fucked up. My bad."

Chocolate Bunny twisted her candy-apple, bright-red painted lips to the side while pulling her dingy G-string out the crack of her wide ass. She knew that Kenya was rolling with Paris and would like nothing better than to see Chocolate Bunny dead or hurt. "Yeah, all right then! And to answer your question, I'm talking about that non-tipping, ancient-dressing asshole Royce!"

"Royce! Royce is in here? Are you sure? Where is he at?" Kenya excitedly scanned the room, hoping she and he could have words.

"Damn, yeah Kenya, I'm sure!" She pointed toward the rear of the club. "He's over there with his crew, talking about he about to buy Alley Cats and trying to get free dances. And you know a good ho like me don't play that free crap no matter who a nigga thinks he is or gonna be! I don't sell free ass this way!"

Before Chocolate Bunny could finish her statement, Kenya had abruptly walked away, leaving her standing alone with the bouncer. *Oh, my God! Maybe Royce knows something about Storm. They was supposed to all be together when they left and O.T. ain't say nothing more about him.* Kenya spotted Royce dressed in one of his 1975 mack-daddy suits and several of his friends seated in the corner, just as Chocolate Bunny said. They had a few bottles of champagne and were surrounded by dancers falling for his weak lines.

"Excuse me, Royce. How you doing?"

"Well, well, well, if it isn't Ms. Tasty."

"Pardon me." Kenya assumed, without a doubt, that she must have been hearing Royce incorrectly.

Royce licked his lips. "Awww . . . Tasty, baby doll, don't be like that! Come over here closer with your pretty little self."

"What did you say?" Kenya felt her world shatter once again. What Royce had just said was hard to digest. No one in Dallas, outside of Storm, O.T., and Deacon knew her as Tasty, not even Paris—that was unless her man had told her.

"Come on now, sweetness. There's no reason to be shy with Daddy." Royce tried rubbing her hand. "I'll give you double if you give me one of your special dances or better yet, go hit that stage. I heard you extra good with a pole between your legs."

"I'm sorry, you must be mistaken. I don't dance. I just came over here to ask you a few questions if you don't mind." Kenya attempted her best to keep her fronts up, knowing she was shook to her soul.

Royce then brazenly pulled out a thick knot of money wrapped in a red rubber band. "You sure you don't want to come out of retirement and make this loot? Ain't nothing but hundreds in this roll and some of it could be yours for the asking, sweet thang you!"

"Listen up, Royce." Kenya was trying her best to remain professional as all eyes were glued on her. "I just need to ask you something in private, if that's okay. You can save the rest of that."

"Why, do you have a wire on you? Did the *Feds* send you to fuck with me or something?"

He stood up from the table with his glass in his hand. Everyone within ear range, drug dealers, dancers, and even the workingman, was quiet waiting for Kenya to respond to the old man's allegations of her working for the police in some capacity. "Now, tsk, tsk tsk. There's no need trying to act naive, young lady. I already know that you play for the other team, so to speak. You snitchin' little tramp! Yeah, I saw the picture. We all did!" Royce raised his left eyebrow, grinning, drink still in hand. "Your man Storm tried denying it, but we all knew. He wasn't slick and you ain't either!"

"What the hell are you insinuating? Storm knew what?" Kenya's violent streak and Detroit-born-and-raised temper was surfacing quickly. She had come to him respectfully, in peace, in hopes of gaining some information on Storm. Now he was calling her out—in her man's club, of all places. "Yeah, all right then." She promptly dismissed the dancers who were idly standing around, not making money but ear hustling. "Y'all girls can leave. This one and his entire crew on they way out the door."

Kenya's teeth were clenched tightly and her lips trembled as she summoned the dancers once more to move on to another customer. They hesitantly did as they were told in a slow fashion, trying to linger around for the shit to hit the fan.

"Hurry the fuck up before I start sending bitches home!" That serious threat of being cut off from the crowd of stuffed pocket men made them speed their departure up. "Now back to you old man! How dare you insult me!" she feverishly lashed out, ready to kill. "All I wanted to find out is if you know anything about Storm. Why are you in here playing games with me? This shit ain't no joke!" Her voice was increasing with every infuriated word. "Are you crazy?"

An equally angry Royce quickly responded. "Pay attention, you little whore! I don't know shit about that coward Deacon or Storm . . . ask Javier, that's your best bet!" He stroked his unshaven salt-and-pepper beard, while straightening out his multicolored polyester suit. His crew were all young in age, yet must have been inspired by their leader when they selected their gear for the evening, all looking like Royce clones. They were hanging on every word that slipped out his past-tense jaws like he was spitting gold. "Matter of fact, here's a better option for you. Why don't you ask the coroner at the local morgue?" Royce boldly suggested, enjoying the growing tension that filled the room. "Yeah, get in touch with them. They probably could answer all your questions better than anyone else. After all, Tasty, Kenya, London or whatever name you're going by tonight, that is where snitches and bitches end up, ain't it—dead in the morgue?"

Kenya was straight bugging out and trembling in denial. Her past was coming back to bite her in the ass. She was completely drained from worry about Storm and sleep deprived. With her body temperature close to reaching boiling level from him exposing her private life to everyone in Alley Cats, her mentality started to further go off into explosive mode. On the other hand, Royce and his friends were taking pleasure in the sight of Kenya's high-and-mighty stuck-up self being brought down a couple of notches to where they felt she belonged. They were still holding their glasses in their hands and smiling, enjoying the show.

Kenya couldn't hold it together any longer. *These busters think I'm here to entertain them. Yeah, all right!* Kenya's mind was racing. Her palms were itching to smack Royce across his unshaven beard. She used her finger to nervously twirl her engagement ring as only one thought monopolized her brain: Storm coming home alive. Now Royce was putting shit in the game, making a scene. "The morgue! What? The morgue! Did I hear you act like you know something about my man? Is that what you doing?"

"You heard what I said, little girl!" With spite, he raised his glass as if he was making a toast.

"Now your best bet is to get the fuck away from me before I kick your period on!"

The crowd was amused by Royce's brash words. Kenya was now borderline psychotic. *Five . . . four . . . three . . . two . . . one*—blast the hell off. Before Royce knew what was happening, Kenya socked him dead in his left eye, followed by several combinations of right and left hooks. He was thrown off balance, falling back into the booth, knocking all the bottles of champagne onto the club floor. Her attack caught his smug crew off guard as they watched Kenya pounce on top of Royce like a sick, deranged mountain lion.

"Motherfucker, you done earned this right here!" she shouted with each blow.

By the time one of his crew could snatch her off of their boss and get him back on his feet, Royce's face was scratched to the white meat. His lip was bleeding and his dentures were hanging sideways out his mouth. Showing no signs of letting up, Kenya wasn't done yet as she struggled to break free and continue showing Royce exactly who was boss in that motherfucker.

"Let me go! Let me go!" Kenya's piercing screams could be heard throughout the whole club. "Let me the fuck go!"

"I'm gonna kill you, slut, just like Javier killed

that no-good snitchin'-ass man of yours!" he boasted once more. Royce's words were vindictive and sliced deep into her inner soul. "Matter of fact, they can bury you both together in a cheap wooden box!"

Kenya broke free of the guy's grip just as O.T. and the bouncers approached them. She stole on Royce once more, this time tagging the other eye. Her perfectly manicured nails had broken off into his face, causing him to scream out like a little baby.

"Don't fold now, old man! I ain't done. Let's do this! Boss the hell up!"

"Y'all better get that wild little whore!" Royce tried commanding his boys, "Before I kill her up in here."

Kenya was on the zigitty nut boom and close to practically foaming at the mouth as Boz grabbed her up in his chest. With Kenya's legs kicking wildly and arms still swinging, Boz caught some serious hell in dragging her up the staircase to the office door. He had easier times trying to throw a grown-ass, six foot two, 300 pound, drunk and disorderly man out of Alley Cats than he was having with his boss's girl.

"I'm gonna get you, Royce! I swear to God, I'm gonna lullaby that old, wrinkled-ass for good one day!" Kenya was leaning over the railing, yelling as an exhausted Boz still struggled. "I swear on everything that I love, just wait! You got that shit coming, Royce! On my parents' grave! That's ya ass!"

"Don't fret, Tasty." Royce was putting on a brave front for the club patrons. His ego was bruised, but he still continued to talk shit, trying his best to save face. "All right girl, I'll see you in them streets real soon and when I do, oh my! I'll teach your pole-swinging-ass a priceless lesson of a lifetime, one that you'll never, ever forget!" Royce blew her a kiss and smiled in spite of the severe pain he was feeling. "I'll see you soon, little girl, real, real soon!"

"Say you promise! You old son of a bitch! Say you motherfucking promise!" Kenya managed to shout recklessly across the crowded bar as Boz finally pried her fingers off the railing and threw her in the office onto the couch, next to her terrified sister.

"Damn, Kenya! What was that all about?" London puzzled, not knowing what to think.

9

Play Ya Position

Kenya confessed to London the real reason that she hadn't mentioned her very existence to her friends and employees. "It's simple. I know that you can't stand drugs or anything affiliated with them, so why would I even wanna get your name mixed into this world that I'm calling home? I mean, be serious, London, I already knew that any hopes of you accepting Storm and his lifestyle was little to none. I ain't stupid."

"Regardless of whatever, Kenya, we're sisters—family—blood. You act as if you're ashamed of me," London argued, feeling some sort of way. "No matter how much foolish stuff you've been caught up in the middle of in the past, I've never turned my back on you or even once thought about it."

"Yeah, you right, London."

"I know I'm right. So there's no reason to be up in here, feeling sorry for yourself. Things are gonna work out, you'll see. Now chill, Kenya, before you have a total nervous breakdown."

Kenya let her body relax and break back down to normal. However, her heart was still racing from her confrontation with Royce. "Girl, I think I better. That old bastard gonna make me hurt him."

"I was watching on that security camera behind the desk over there." London smiled, knowing how her twin could get when pushed to the edge or backed into a corner. "You are in some serious need of anger management. I'm telling you, Kenya, you are a straight-up nutcase."

"I know sis. I think I picked up some of your bad habits."

London hugged her twin, trying to ease her pain and worry. "You wish!"

Much to Kenya's surprise, during the course of their conversation, London announced to her that after long consideration, she'd reluctantly decided to at least return the 15,000-dollar gift that her twin had blessed her with.

"Thank you, sis. I knew that you wasn't gonna just leave me hanging like that. You best believe that I wouldn't even think about being an Indian giver if it wasn't a doggone emergency." Kenya was counting every penny she got her hands on, as a penny closer to Storm's release.

"Stop that kinda talk. I'll call my bank sometime tomorrow and get the money wired out
here, okay?"

"Thanks, London."

"We're sisters, girl. I love you."

Meantime, O.T. was left to settle up and iron
things out with a half-crazed, wounded physically and emotionally Royce. "Man, what the
fuck did you say to piss her off like that?"

"What the hell you mean, what did I say?"
Royce quizzed, hunching his shoulders, wiping
the blood out the side corner of his swollen lip.
"That silly once-a-month-bleeding bitch just
went bananas for no good reason at all! She
needs to be fucking medicated or put down!"

O.T. quickly studied the faces of Royce's
crew as they listened to their self-proclaimed
leader punk out. They, along with several of
the dancers and patrons, were stricken with
amazement; that after blowing all that old-style
wannabe-gangster bullshit out his busted grill,
Royce was standing in O.T.'s face taking a cop
to his snide comments, hurtful open-ended
threats, and incredible accusations about the
club's owner, O.T.'s brother.

"Damn, dawg, it's like that?" O.T. turned his
fitted baseball cap backwards, getting in

his zone. He cracked his knuckles while slightly smirking. Beads of sweat were swiftly forming on his forehead. "Please don't let me even imagine that your ass is truly gonna go out like this! I ain't trying to act no fool up in here and ruin none of these hardworking folks' night!"

The bouncers, ten deep, were all posted, ready to attack just in case O.T. needed backup.

"Come on now. What you talking about, youngblood? Where you going with all this?" Royce was shaking in his burgundy and yellow two-toned Stacy Adams as his crew put some cowardly space in between him and O.T.

When the shit jumped and the fists started to fly, it was more than apparent Royce was gonna be on his own on this one. This was potentially gonna be one stump down that his old-school-ass had coming. He had no business coming up in Storm's club, of all places, beefing with his girl, talking all that la-la-la mess. He'd crossed the line on number one of the player's code of ethics. Now, for real, for real, flat the fuck out, it was on! He had to pay up.

A bigger crowd started also gathered around the booth after the DJ stopped spinning music. Most of the dancers held their G-strings in their hands and had stopped giving private dances to eyewitness Royce get put back in his place. Even Chocolate Bunny's hard-hustlin' behind was waiting for the come on to come on and she wouldn't let the pope himself or Jesus slow her cash flow.

The entire town knew that O.T. was on lunatic status; a true, legendary madman when it came to clowning. And knew he was a few seconds shy of putting on a real show for all those who cared to see. A show so worthy that the streets would be buzzing about it for months and months to follow.

"Well, what's it gonna be, Royce? You plan on being a man and pulling your panties out your ass or what? How you wanna handle this bull-shit? You gonna be a man or is we straight about to get gangsta with it?"

"Come on now, O.T., sit down and have a drink with me, youngblood. Can't we handle this misunderstanding like two gentlemen? I mean player to player, pimp to pimp?" Royce was trying his hardest to backpedal and talk his way out of the situation at hand.

O.T. had blood in his eyes as he spoke. "Listen here, pops, I wanna work with ya, but I ain't gonna be able to." He frowned as his cheekbone twitched and he posted up seconds away from attacking. "The question is still on the table. You gonna have some balls and 'fess up or what? Trust me, Royce! This is the final time a nigga like me gonna ask a ho-ass nigga like you! Trust when I warn you, you think my sister-in law Kenya whooped that ass, you ain't seen shit yet!"

"Okay, okay, okay!" Royce pleaded, throwing his hands up in hopes of buying a few more minutes, stalling a beat-down. "Just pump ya brakes, O.T., let me explain, but I guarantee you want to hear what I have to say in private. Please, man, for old time's sake? How about it?" Royce, having lost all pride, begged relentlessly.

"Yeah, okay then. I'm gonna hear you out and this shit better be good!" O.T. collared Royce up by his oversized lapels. "We can talk over there at my private table. Ya ho-ass boys can wait here or out in the parking lot! I don't give a shit!"

Royce was passed embarrassed, but still tried to save face and delegate some authority with O.T.'s huge hands firmly wrapped around his throat. "Y'all dudes can chill over here. I'll be back." Hopefully he would save himself the possibility of having to drink his food outta a straw for the next six months.

His crew, like everyone else in Alley Cats, had to laugh. Not only had Kenya and O.T. made a fool of him, now he was doing it to himself. It was official—Royce was a class-A idiot and all of Dallas knew it.

After nearly an entire hour of listening to Royce talk, explain, take a cop, and lie, O.T. was even more heated. He couldn't believe what he was hearing the old man claiming. Royce was right. This was the type of information that shouldn't be made public. Yet, in reality, he knew this was the first time Royce had probably repeated the outrageous story.

"Come on now, Royce, how many people you done told this story to? And try your best not to motherfucking lie!"

"To be honest with you, youngblood, only my boys over there know about it." He nodded toward their general direction. "And I've already told them to keep it close to the vest."

"Damn, Royce! Good looking out." O.T. was playing the game. He wasn't dumb. He knew good and goddamn well that if Royce hadn't already told the entire town of Dallas, he was well on his way; especially after tonight. After all, truth be told, if he or Storm had that type of dirt on Royce, you best believe that all bets would've been off.

"No problem, youngblood. We in this here game as us against the man. We gotta stick together."

O.T. was fed up with Royce's ass-kissing, but he was glad that he'd at least heard Royce's tainted version of what really went down with his brother, Deacon, and Javier on the island. From the pictures of London Roberts, one of the cofounders of P.A.I.D., being passed around the table, to Storm's initial shock of seeing them, realizing that his woman was playing both sides to the middle. However, not wanting to throw his own self under the bus, Royce failed to mention to O.T. that he was the first one to put his brother on blast. Not wanting any more hand-to-face confrontation, he wised-up. He didn't want to risk getting beat-down again, so he conveniently left that part out of the story.

Royce went on to explain how Javier had both Storm and Deacon physically removed from the round table. He confessed that he and others heard a lot of hollering and commotion from inside the villa as he and the men were dismissed for the day. "Listen, real talk. I even tried reasoning with Javier, telling him that your brother wasn't like that and it had to be some sort of a mistake, but Javier wasn't trying to hear it." Royce threw that lie in the conversation, trying to throw O.T. off his scent of bullshit. "The next thing I can recall was two days later, Javier summoned us all back to the round table and dropped some knowledge on us."

"Oh, yeah, go on with it." O.T. was on the edge of the booth, listening in amazement.

Royce reached for a napkin to wipe the still slow-dripping blood off his lip that was continuing to throb as time ticked by. "As I was saying, Javier informed us that the hit man named Swift, or something like that, he sent out to Detroit to assassinate London Roberts, had the tables turned on him and he himself been murdered." Royce paused to catch his breath. "Apparently, not only is your brother's woman a straight-up crazed bitch living a double life, she's hooked up somehow with a radical group in Detroit that calls themselves the Motown Muslim Mafia. They must be powerful as hell with they shit, because one of their members who goes by the name Brother Rasul, had Swift's body shipped COD to Javier's front door with a note attached to his torso. I mean, that's the word that was floating around that man's compound."

Mentioning the Detroit-based hard hitters that Kenya and London were mixed up with caused O.T. to be silent, listening to Royce's deadly tale of what could possibly have been his big brother's last days on Earth. Royce could see the look of worry on O.T.'s face and decided to play his act for all that it was worth. He knew that he had to do a lot of fast talking and expert acting to convince O.T. to let him walk out of Alley Cats in one piece. Royce kept it coming.

"Now, I don't know what exactly were the contents of the letter word for word, but I do know that Javier stated that a horrible mistake had been made and asked us all to vacate the island by nightfall. He generously gave us each a half a kilo of his finest product uncut, having us to swear to keep the situation under wraps until further notice. That's it!" Royce grabbed for another napkin, trying to absorb the pouring sweat mixed with blood from his aging face. "No more was brought up about Deacon or Storm's whereabouts and who was I to question that man? A few hours later we were all put on a private jet and flown back to the States."

"Just like that?" O.T. sat, amazed at the wild tale he'd just heard.

"Sorry I couldn't have given you more encouraging news about Storm's well-being, but from where I stood, it didn't seem too pretty. But, one thing for sure, two things for certain, Javier seems to be very calculated about every single move he makes and words he speaks, so don't give up hope, youngblood. Anything is possible."

O.T. chose not to drop his hand, letting Royce's backstabbing-ass in on the fact that he'd already been in contact with Javier and if things went as planned, Storm would soon be returning home. Bottom line, you never let the left know what the right is doing. With authority, he then signaled to Boz to escort Royce and his entire crew to the door. Before leaving, O.T. made sure to make it perfectly clear that he was interested in buying some of that high-quality dope that Royce claimed he was sitting on. Royce quickly agreed, knowing that if he didn't, it would more than likely be an all-out open drug war in the streets of Dallas. His hands were tied tight.

Royce might have dressed like a clown and fight like a bitch, but he was a true businessman and it was to his benefit to make money, not mayhem. He really couldn't care less where the drugs were being sold at as long as he got his money off top. What did he care about—as far as he knew Storm and Deacon were both dead; so that meant he was about to rule the city one day soon.

Now O.T. was a hothead and extremely arrogant about his shit, vowing to die first before letting other crews violate the blocks that him or his big brother ran with iron fists. A fool would be signing their own death certificate if they ever tried. Always down for whatever it took, he didn't give a shit about it being only two or three burn bags that a dopefiend was trying to get off, O.T. always kept it gangsta.

Those blocks belonged to them, point-blank, period, end of fucking story! You feel me! Case closed!

10

Paid In Full

London and Kenya left Alley Cats that night, staying pretty much secluded in the confines of the hotel until the repairmen had the condo back in livable condition. O.T. delivered the profits from each night at the club and the loot that he made from other ventures here and there. Staying true to his ways, he made sure to flirt with London on every occasion he saw her. Kenya, not blind or naive, noticed an increasing change in her sister's behavior every time he'd stop by their suite. London was acting overly sassy and out of character.

On the day the girls finally returned to the condo, Kenya was a bit worried her home, which people once described as a masterpiece, would not be repaired properly. When the sisters originally crossed the threshold of the door, Kenya took a long whiff, trying to see if she could smell the scent of death in the air.

She rubbed her chin, trying to figure out the difference between fresh paint and plaster and the everlasting, imaginary stench of Deacon's lifeless corpse.

Taking a tour around her home, inspecting the workmanship, left Kenya having flashbacks of her and Storm's once perfect life. The stainless-steel sink was clean and the kitchen cabinets were all freshly varnished. New appliances lined the walls. The floors had custom-made marble that reached clear out to the patio deck. With the brand-new living room set, along with the rest of the other overpriced furniture she charged on credit, Kenya was somewhat at peace.

It was bad enough that Kenya had to live with the feeling of being violated, by strangers being in her private sanctuary, but she had no intentions of keeping not one stick of butter they might have touched. Even though some of the condo contents could be salvaged, Kenya wasn't interested. She wanted no reminders of their trespassing presence whatsoever.

"Is everything okay?" London watched as her twin slowly made her survey.

"Yeah, I'm tight," Kenya sighed. "I was just thinking about the days that we have left to hustle up on the funds we need." It was eleven days and counting and they were still short by 48,000 dollars.

***

Although Storm preached repeatedly, time and time again to his baby brother, about hanging out, chillin' in the dope spots, and actually making hand-to-hand transactions, at that point it didn't matter. O.T. stayed in the streets slinging dope, night after night, sunup to sundown . . . he hustled. Everyone knew if you broke a package down and sold it, you'd make double, maybe even triple, what you originally paid. The risk was high, but the payoff was lovely.

Paris was missing her man, especially at late night when she wanted some, but she had her own task: holding Alley Cats down. Caught up in being an almost one-woman hustling army, she had drink specials running all night long, even letting the fattest, ugliest girls shake their asses on the big moneymaking days. As long as a chick could come up on the house fee, which was raised to a hundred dollars a night, they were good to go. Everyone was doing their part to get Storm, whether they knew it or not.

Paris's patience as temporary club manager was being put to the test on a daily basis by the increasingly arrogant actions of Chocolate Bunny, who ho-hopped around Alley Cats as if she owned the motherfucker or had stock. Lately, whenever O.T. came into the club, Paris would find him tucked away in some corner of the bar, whispering in Chocolate Bunny's big floppy ears. As far as Paris was concerned, she wanted her man to barely speak to the chicks who danced there, shaking they asses, then keep that shit moving. Breaking the house rules, to Chocolate Bunny, weren't by accident—they were more like a force of habit. Fighting back the urge to snap, Paris held her tongue for the good of Storm's safe return. Yet, she knew in the back of her mind as soon as he returned home, her claws would come out and she was gonna wax the floor with Chocolate Bunny's face.

Back home in Detroit, the real estate agent had contacted the twins, informing them that there was some sort of holdup in the transferring of the deed to Gran's house and there would be a thirty-to forty-five-day delay in the closing process. Sadly, any thoughts of relying on that cash revenue to push them past their needed goal were ceased. It seemed as if that house was cursed all the way around.

Just as Kenya put her hand around the brass-plated banister to go upstairs, her cell phone rang. "Hello."

"*As-salaam alaikum*, Kenya. Is this you?"

"Brother Rasul! Brother Rasul!" Kenya was elated as she smiled from ear to ear. "I'm so glad to hear from you. I wanted to get in touch with you ever since we got back in Dallas, but I knew better. Plus, so much been going on!"

"Al hamd li Allah," Brother Rasul added to his greeting.

"Praise be to Allah," Kenya repeated to him, calming herself down.

London ran to her sister's side. "Is that your friend? Is Fatima with him? Is she?" She grabbed for the phone. "Can I speak to her?"

Brother Rasul heard all the questions. "Tell her that Fatima is back up at the university and sends her very best wishes. She wanted to call London personally, but I also explained to her that it would be best to lay low until I got to the bottom of all of this madness."

London was close enough to the cell phone to hear what the man who had saved their lives said. She believed in him for some strange reason. After all, Brother Rasul did put his own safety and freedom on the line for them and for that he forever earned her trust and respect. She was eternally grateful.

"I'm glad that you did as I told you and waited for me to get in touch with you," he praised her patience. "That was indeed the best plan of action."

"Oh, Brother Rasul, so much chaos has happened since we got here. We came home to find, Deacon, my fiancé's partner, dead in my house and some crazy son of a bitch is holding Storm hostage until we—"

"Until you come up with two hundred and fifty thousand dollars." Brother Rasul finished a shocked Kenya's sentence. "I was thoroughly informed pertaining that situation."

"Who told you? How did you find out?"

"Whoa, slow down, little sister. I told you I was gonna investigate the man-in-the-house situation and I did just that. Apparently, they go hand in hand with your present dilemma."

"Oh, my God! Oh, my God! Did you find out any information about Storm? Is he okay? Did you speak to him?" Kenya sobbed, shaking from nervousness. "Please say yes—please!"

"Well, yes and no." A calm-voiced Brother Rasul went over his conversation that just had taken place, less than a hour ago, between him and Javier. "It seems as if your friend's host, turned kidnapper, was first infuriated at the actions of Fatima and your sister London. Apparently, their widespread organization P.A.I.D. caused a lot of financial downfalls for quite a few slimy lowlife drug dealers infesting the neighborhoods and killing our greatest resource, kids. The marches on drug houses caused many to shut down. It's one thing to sell drugs, but not to pregnant women and underage children. That's where me and my people draw the line"

"Oh, I see," Kenya interjected, feeling ashamed that Storm was one of the "anybody can buy" drug dealers that Brother Rasul was referring to. But nevertheless, she still wanted him home safe and sound. The world be damned about their point of views.

"Well, Kenya, after sending one of his henchmen, Swift, to Detroit to execute this London Roberts person, he somehow came to find out that Storm had been dating her. It seems as if Javier and everyone who was in attendance at this meeting, who saw the pictures being passed around for the first time, assumed it was you, Kenya, aka London Roberts. Do you understand what I'm saying?"

Kenya's mind flashed back to the altercation that she had in Alley Cats. At that point it didn't take a brain surgeon to figure the whole thing out. Kenya couldn't avoid the truth any longer, even if she wanted to. This was concrete evidence that Brother Rasul had gotten straight from the horse's mouth and it was crystal clear. *Now it made sense what Royce meant when he called me a snitchin'-ass bitch. Damn, that's why that fool called me London. Oh, fuck! He*

*must have seen the pictures and thought that
she was working with the police. I mean, he
thought that I was. Damn!* She started to hyperventilate and wheeze when it hit her. The
two worlds Kenya systematically did her best to
keep apart, were now colliding. Then the next
alarm rang in her head. *Oh, shit! If Royce's ass
saw those pictures, then I know that Storm
must've seen them too. Oh, my God! I can't believe this! I know he must be going half out his
mind. My baby probably thinks that I betrayed
him. He must hate me right about now! Why
didn't I just be honest and tell him from the
get-go—why?*

London took the cell out of her panicked
sister's hand. "Hello. Hey now, this is London."

"Hello, London. Where is Kenya? What
happened?"

London glanced over at a blank-faced-
looking Kenya and answered Brother Rasul's
question. "I'm sorry, but you should know how
she is by now. You know Kenya overreacts with
everything she says and does. She's playing the
drama queen right now, of all times."

"Come on, London. That's your sister. You
have to realize that she's going through a difficult and trying time in her life now. So give
her a break." Brother Rasul was acting as both
peacemaker and therapist.

London listened to Brother Rasul's speech with growing anger, almost wanting to throw up in her mouth. The feeling of animosity toward Kenya and the whole mess was fueling her outburst. "I know she's catching it right now, not knowing if Storm is alive or not, but what about me? Who's feeling any sympathy for my plight?" London was visibly enraged as her impromptu rant continued. "I should be back at school with Fatima, working on my degree, not stuck here playing Inspector Gadget for some dope dealer!"

For the first time since being in Dallas, London was determined to make someone hear and understand her point of view. Playing the background dummy was over. It was her time to vent and get some things off her chest. Caught in her emotions, enraged, she went on and on, not giving Brother Rasul a second to get a word in edgewise. As London was almost out of breath from all of her screaming, O.T. entered the room. She saw him coming out the corner of her eye and decided to pour it on extra-thick.

"No one loves or cares about me! What about me?" she sobbed out loud, as the fake tears flowed, dropping the cell phone to the carpeted floor. "Who's going to look out for me and my future? I'm scared too! What about me?"

O.T. reached down, picking up the phone and yanking London into his body in one quick motion. "What's wrong? What's the deal, baby girl?" O.T. wrapped his arms around London's waist. "Tell me and what's wrong with your sister?"

London continued to play the weak role as O.T. finally spoke to the person on the other end of the phone.

"Yeah, hello! Hello!" He was impatient for a response as he kept a clinging, calculating London in his arms.

"Peace. Whom am I speaking to?" Brother Rasul remained, as always, even-toned.

"This is O.T., who this?"

"My name is Brother Rasul Hakim Akbar. I am a close friend of the girls."

O.T. loosened his grip on London, realizing who he was speaking to and the power that Royce mentioned that this man held. "Brother Rasul. I've heard of you."

"I trust that it was all positive and uplifting, but in all fairness I must admit that I don't know you." Brother Rasul was respectful, yet guarded, as he spoke to this stranger. He had no intentions of socializing with just anyone. "Can you please let me speak back to one of the twins? We have a bit of unfinished business that I need to inform them of."

"No problem, dude, but first I need to know if you know anything about my brother's whereabouts?"

"And just who is your brother?"

"His name is Tony Christian, but he goes by the name Storm. He's Kenya's man! I know you've heard of him!" O.T. was tired of all the formalities and went straight to it. "Look, I already know you down with them Motown Muslim Mafia cats! I know y'all bodied that nigga Swift that tried to do Kenya and London." O.T. rubbed his hands across London's wet face and drew her back close to him. "Tell him I'm official, London. Tell him it's all good."

London leaned her cheek next to O.T.'s. "Hey, Brother Rasul. This is Storm's brother. He's been helping us and making sure that we stay safe." London made sure to mimic Kenya, trying to look sexy and seductive as she spoke. She softly bit the side of her lip just as Kenya often did to get her way with a man.

"Okay then, little one, I'll tell him what I wanted to put Kenya up on," Brother Rasul agreed.

O.T. was all ears. "All right, guy. You heard her, now please tell me what you know about my brother. Is he still alive or what? What's the real deal? Raw or not, I need the truth!"

"Well, I just got off the phone with Javier. He told me that he gave your family thirty days to come up with two hundred and fifty thousand dollars. Is that correct?"

"Yeah, that's right," O.T. huffed, "And that's some bullshit, straight-up extortion!"

"I know. That price is a little steep, even if Javier feels like he's been wronged somehow."

"Wronged how? Storm didn't know shit about all that P.A.I.D. crap y'all keep talking about." O.T. walked to the other side of the room away from London. "How is he to blame? Tell me that much—how?"

Brother Rasul could feel O.T.'s intense fury over the phone. "Listen, brother, I'm not calling to discuss who's right or who's wrong or who owes who what. My organization tries not to get involved in the drug game on a daily basis. That's not our main objective. We have other concerns." Brother Rasul finally dropped the bomb, putting O.T. out his misery. "I just wanted to let Kenya know that I settled up the rest of the debt that Javier was strong-arming you all out of."

"What exactly does that mean, dude? Cut all the cloak-and-dagger out!" O.T. was confused and wanted some answers in plain English, straight to the point. "What you mean, *settled up*?"

"What it means is Javier has given me his word as a gentleman that in less than forty-eight hours, your brother Storm will be released and returned home."

"Are you for real? Don't be fucking around with my emotions!" O.T. blurted into the phone, causing Kenya to shake off her self-induced pity-party trance and run toward O.T., pushing London aside.

"Yes, Javier reassured me. And he knows that we as a whole don't take pleasure in being lied to," Brother Rasul snarled. "I know that you are overjoyed, O.T., but slow down, there's been some discomfort and pain that your brother has been made to suffer, so please prepare yourself, as well as Kenya."

"I know. That old, crazy dude sliced part of my brother's earlobe off."

"I was made aware of that. However, I'm afraid that it's a little bit worse than what you think."

"How much more worse?" O.T. hesitated asking, fearing the answer.

"Listen, the damage had already been inflicted before we got involved. It was nothing that I could have done or said to have prevented it. Just tell Kenya to remain strong and to call me if need be. Peace."

O.T. flipped closed the cell and led the girls into the living room, sitting them both down on the couch.

"Well, O.T., what did he say? Is Storm coming home soon? Has Javier changed his mind or something?" Kenya, acting extra, held onto his hand, squeezing it extra-tightly, jumping back up. "What did he say?"

"Sit back down, Kenya and pay attention. This shit here is deep."

"Yeah Kenya, damn, sit down!" London added, watching O.T. like a hawk. "Let him finish speaking, for God's sake!"

A bitter, yet thankful O.T. tried to the best of his ability to prepare Kenya for the unknown circumstances of Storm's arrival, even though he wasn't truly sure himself of what condition they'd get his beloved brother back. All he knew was he was still alive and that was good enough for him.

11

Done is Done

"It's six hours short of the deadline that Brother Rasul said." Kenya anxiously paced the floor. "I wonder, should I call him back and see what the problem is?"

"Naw, Kenya, don't call him yet. He said Javier gave him his word, so let's just ride it out and see. We done waited this long, we can go another six."

"Okay, O.T, but one second after six hours and I'm calling, flat out." Kenya's palms were sweaty as she wore a path in the carpet from the door to the window and the window to the couch.

London, Paris, Kenya, and O.T. were all posted, congregated in the front room watching the wall clock move slowly. It was like sheer torture for the group, waiting and wondering what Storm's physical and mental condition was going to be. As the clock ticked, their fears increased, awaiting the unexpected to occur.

Kenya, having the most to lose, was on edge more than anyone else in the house. Storm was her life. She felt without him she was nothing. As the clock slowly dragged by, the tension could be cut with a knife. You could almost hear a tiny pin drop if you listened carefully. It seemed as if every fifteen minutes the silence was broken by O.T.'s cell phone constantly ringing. Even after turning it to vibrate it could still be heard in the midst of the quiet that surrounded the room. Each time he would look down at the screen and see the caller ID, he got more visibly agitated.

Paris and his arguing had increased a lot over the last few weeks, because she knew deep down in her heart, despite his denials, that he was up to no good. "I wish that disrespectful bitch of yours would stop blowing up the damn phone for once!" Paris blurted out with jealous malice. "Don't she ever sleep? All day and all fucking night!" she went on a long-winded rant. "Tell that cheap ho to get herself a life and go find her own man!"

"Look, girl, I already done told your silly, insecure-ass that I ain't fucking around with nobody else, so stop all that bugging." O.T. kissed Paris on her forehead as she pulled away. "So just chill the hell out, crazy. Ain't nobody getting Daddy's dick but you!"

"Whatever liar! Go on with all that game!"

Paris didn't believe him one bit, just as London, who felt jealous and somehow betrayed. It was bad enough in her eyes that he was claiming Paris as number one, but now she had some other uneducated loser as competition for his rotten affections.

Why is he doing this? He knows I like him. London's mind went over and over the reason in her head a million times as she watched, envious of the couple's twisted yet loving interactions. It was making her downright sick to her stomach.

"Can y'all all just shut the fuck up for a minute and put that stuff on the back burner? Y'all making me even more nervous, shit!" Kenya halted the heated argument between the two, with rage in her voice. "I can't think!"

"Yeah, can you two please be quiet?" London was quick to jump to her sister's defense, although she had her own secret, ulterior motives. "As much as I hate to interrupt your exchange, this isn't the time or the place to discuss your intimate personal problems."

Everyone agreed as London turned the radio onto a jazz station she'd found, coaxing them to try to relax. She then disappeared into the kitchen to fix some coffee for the group that was all on edge. *Maybe everyone will calm down,* London thought as she ran some water.

She put the kettle on the stove, turning the fire on high. After getting some mugs out of the cabinets and rinsing them all out, London felt chills rush throughout her body as a pair of big, strong hands firmly gripped her waist. She could feel the warmth of O.T.'s breath in her ear as he whispered.

"Hey now, sexy. What you in here doing all by yourself?" O.T. devilishly smiled.

London's legs were growing weak as she tried to speak, but couldn't. Turning her body around with ease, O.T. pressed his tongue deep into London's mouth. His dick was hard as a rock as he shoved her up against the sink and started to slow grind. London was, for the first time, feeling raw-dog nasty-ass passion. Even though, thanks to the brutal rape she suffered at the hands of her devious college professor—meaning she was no longer a virgin—she still was unaware of what she was feeling.

Her pussy seemed to have a voice of its own and was calling out to O.T. to answer. London was feeling a true out-of-body experience and felt bigger than life itself. The fact that Paris and Kenya were merely yards away in the next room only added to the thrill and sheer excitement that the two were creating. The kettle was getting hotter and coming to a boil just as both of them were.

***

"I'm sorry about all that, girl, but I know that nigga is back fooling around with Chocolate Bunny's behind. They always be exchanging funny looks and notes and shit almost every night. My homegirl Jordan, from down at the club, said that black bitch has been going around bragging about some new buster that she done hooked up with." Paris seized the opportunity to gossip and fill Kenya in about her recent dilemma as soon as O.T. excused himself to go to the bathroom. "Jordan even told me that brain-dead cum-drunk Chocolate Bunny has been flashing a big-ass motherfucking ring somebody put on that bird's finger—I mean claw!"

"Shut the fuck up, Paris! Don't play with me, girl! I know that nigga ain't barebacking down with that wilded-out tramp again!" Kenya momentarily forgot about her own problems for a hot second and joined her friend in talking about O.T.'s known cheating ways. "That fool ain't lost his mind! He knows that ya ass will kill them both and then bounce!"

"Girl, he better not let me find out for sure they screwing, because if I do I swear I'm done! That's my word!" Paris's troubled relationship was in limbo and on the verge of ruin. Folding her arms in disgust, she sat back quietly, puzzling where she went wrong with O.T.

Kenya regretted the fact that her twin sister was attracted to O.T. and knew, given the right amount of time or the right circumstance, the two would probably act on that emotion. She was shocked that Paris, usually perceptive about these types of things when it came to her man, couldn't pick up on it. Her woman's-intuition radar must've been broken. Even Ray Charles on a bad day could see the way her sister and he carried on at all times. It was definitely a thin line between love and hate going on.

Oh, shit! Noticing O.T. was taking a long time returning from the bathroom, Kenya jumped to her feet and ran into the kitchen. Her intuition was working just fine!

The kettle started to whistle a long, piercing sound as Kenya abruptly entered the kitchen. "What the fuck are y'all doing?" She jerked her sister and her best friend's man apart. "Have y'all two lost y'all's mind or something? I know you are both aware that Paris is right in there." Kenya pointed toward the living room, trying her best to whisper. "O.T.! Why would you jeopardize getting caught and risk losing your woman? Is all this creeping shit you always doing worth it?"

Kenya, directing all her questions toward him, gave London a chance to remove the loud-sounding kettle from the stove.

"Dang, Kenya, why don't you chill with all that talk? You must want us to get caught up and shit!" O.T. laughed, placing his index finger up to his lips. Without any remorse, he headed back out to the living room. "I'll be in there with my baby, Paris."

Kenya was infuriated with London. That was the final straw. "Have you lost your damn mind? What the hell has gotten into your sneaky-ass lately? This kinda crap don't make any freaking sense! Do I have to remind you that Paris is my damn friend—my best friend at that?"

"No, Kenya, no you don't!" London was up in Kenya's face, fist balled on the verge of swinging. "That's all the hell I've been hearing ever since I got here in Dallas. Paris this and Paris that. Well, I'm sick of it! So there! Fuck Paris and you! Y'all can have each other—I'm good!"

Kenya was thrown off by the fact that her sister was cursing and all up in her face as if she was ready to attack a bitch. "Oh, it's like that now?" Kenya grinned, braced to swing back on her sister if need be. "I guess you's a big girl, huh? You wanna do big-girl shit—is that right?"

"Yeah, it's just like that!" London refused to back down this time as the twins stood toe-to-toe. "So now what are you going to do, Miss Drama Queen? I'm not scared or ashamed, so go ahead and do what you gotta do!"

Paris, as if on cue, walked in the kitchen just in time to stop the girls from coming to blows. "Hey, what's wrong in here? Y'all act like y'all about to throw down."

"Nothing," the twins answered at the same time.

Collectively, they put their family argument on hold as all three of the girls rejoined a smug-faced O.T. in the living room, waiting for Storm's arrival.

Kenya, tired of watching her sister and O.T. give each other the side eye on the sly, grew fed up and was about to explode and spill the beans, letting the chips fall where they may. "You know what?" she asked, looking at Paris with her eyes bucked and lips pouted out.

Before Paris got a chance to reply, there was a soft knock at the front door, causing everyone to pause and fortunately stopping an overly frustrated Kenya from busting on O.T. and her sister. Getting up, pulling his pistol out of his waistband, he put one up top. O.T. signaled over to his soon-to-be sister-in-law to get ready.

"All right, Kenya. Go ahead—open up the door!"

Kenya turned the knob on the door and cautiously pulled it open. She peeked out, barely getting a glimpse of the tail end of a black Yukon driving off as quietly as it apparently had driven up. Kenya looked down, receiving a happy, but sad, sight. Her man was home. It was Storm laid out on the front porch. His back was turned away from her, but Kenya could tell that it was without a doubt him. It was her Storm and he was home. Now things could possibly go back to normal and all would be well.

"O.T., hurry up! It's Storm! He needs help!"

Paris and O.T. ran out onto the stairs, leaving a hesitant London standing alone, waiting to come face-to-face with the all-so famous Storm. Even though she helped out in giving up her money for his safe return, she didn't know him, so it was hard for her to show genuine concern.

O.T. placed his hand on his brother's shoulder and took his time carefully turning him over on his back. "That motherfucker! That old motherfucker!" O.T. mumbled with Javier on his mind. He was pissed to see his brother looking like he did. Paris, distraught, covered her mouth in total disbelief, while Kenya's already fragile heart skipped a beat and crumbled at the sight of her once strong, handsome, devoted fiancé all the girls wanted to be with and who all the guys wanted to be.

"How could they?" Kenya buried her face, sobbing into her hands. "Why would they—why?"

Storm's face had been somewhat mutilated and disfigured. Not only was his earlobe sliced, his entire right side of his jaw was bigger than both Kenya's hands put together. His once-perfect, kissable lips were cracked and dry as if he hadn't had water or any other fluids in days on end. Storm's overall body weight was decreased by at least twenty pounds since Kenya and O.T. last saw him. His left leg had a makeshift kind of medical bandage attached to a flimsy basement-made splint. And lastly, Storm was delirious and beyond dazed.

"Come on, y'all, and help me get him inside before the nosy-ass neighbors around here come outside," O.T. loudly ordered. "We have to get him on the couch and off this hard, cold concrete."

Paris let her anger with O.T. go as she bent down, positioning herself to help lift an almost motionless Storm up. "Kenya, we need you to get on his other side so we won't bump his leg. Hurry up, because I'm losing my grip."

Standing frozen momentarily, Kenya swiftly snapped back to reality and took Storm's twisted leg in her arms. London could see that the trio was struggling, so she rushed over, swinging the door open wide as she could, praying to score points with O.T. for helping. When they got a semiconscious Storm on the couch, turning all the lights on brightly, they got a chance to fully take in the true harshness of the way that Storm was treated wherever he was being held captive at.

Storm's eyes were puffy, red, and watery. Almost swollen shut in the corners, they kept rolling in the back of his head while he was mumbling words that made absolutely no sense whatsoever to any of them. It was as if he was what the old people down south called "speaking in tongues" or "talking out the side of his neck," like he was insane. It was obvious he was half out of his mind.

Oh, my God! This is bad! London thought.

Storm was drifting in and out of consciousness. The once-vibrant, outgoing young man wasn't aware of his surroundings or any of his family around him. Storm was messed up bad, to put it mildly!

"That fried-bean-eating motherfucker Javier is gonna pay for this! I don't give a shit how long it takes! Ain't nan son of a bitch alive walking this damn earth gonna do this type of bullshit to my family and live long to brag about it!" O.T. kicked the end table, causing the lamp to wobble. "I swear I mean it! I swear I do!"

"Listen, baby," Paris reassuringly caressed his back as she tried to soften his fury. "Now is not the time to trip. We should be thanking God that we didn't get Storm back in a body bag! Now we gotta call somebody and get your brother some medical attention. That's first on the agenda. So snap outta it and let's get it done!"

Remembering how Deacon made it back home, headless, London agreed with Paris as they stood on each side of O.T., watching Kenya down on her knees, kissing Storm's swollen face. "I'm so sorry, baby," she repeated as she wet his split lip with a moist rag. "So, so sorry."

"He knows already, Kenya," Paris now consoled her best friend also. "He knows, girl—he knows."

O.T. flipped open his phone and strolled down his locked-in contact numbers. He went down a long, long list until he found it. "Here it is!" he announced, happily glancing over at his injured brother. "Bernard Crayton." O.T. waited for the person to answer his call. "Hey dude, this is O.T., I need you to do me a solid. ASAP. It's an emergency—a serious one!"

"From the looks of things, without the aid of X-rays, it seems as if Storm's leg is broken. Now, considering the swelling and the color tone of the bruises on the lower knee area, I think it's already started the healing process, but honestly, in my opinion, if it isn't put in a cast and set properly, he might end up with a permanent limp."

Dr. Bernard S. Crayton had gotten to the condo in less than twenty minutes after O.T. placed the call to him. He was a regular fixture down at Alley Cats and on call 24-7 anytime one of the fellas would need him. He was a licensed plastic surgeon by trade, but treated everything from a hangnail on a cat to one of the hot box dancers at the club who was running around setting all the VIP customers' dicks on fire. Big Doc B, as everyone called him, would write a bitch a prescription for having a bad hair day if she paid him enough. He was shady as a motherfucker could get, but knew his shit. "Come on, let's move him to a bed and get him undressed so that I can examine him fully and get a better look at the damage."

As Kenya led the way, O.T. and Big Doc B carried the completely passed out Storm up to the bedroom.

"Lay him down here." She yanked back the covers and started undressing Storm the best she could as the guys talked over on the other side of the newly decorated master suite. Using scissors, she cut away what was too difficult to remove.

"You know that all this shit is on the hush-hush right?" O.T. focused in on Big Doc B's eyes.

"Come on now, how you gonna play me? You know me better than that," the doctor reassured him. "I know the routine."

"You my nigga!" O.T. smiled, placing one hand on his shoulder. "My motherfucking nigga!"

London and Paris were now left standing alone downstairs once again. It was much like the night that the two had first met, only this time the victim in the house was Storm instead of Deacon.

"I wonder what's going on up there? I hope he's all right." Paris put her hand on her chest. "I know Kenya is tripping out right about now."

"I know. I've been on my knees praying every night that Storm was safe." London was lying through her teeth as she tried conniving in intent to befriend Paris. "I know that O.T. is happy. Maybe now you two can stop all that silly bickering and live happily ever after."

Paris went and plopped down in the chair, feeling the brand-new soft, buttery leather. "Naw London, I'm afraid that it's a little bit deeper than just Storm being gone. Me and that man been and still do got bigger issues than that—much bigger!"

"Dang, gee Paris, I'm sorry to hear that." London smirked behind Paris's back. "Do you want to talk about it? I'm a good listener."

"Nope, I'm tight. I'm good. Besides, I ain't trying to start crying."

"Girl, maybe you should just get it off your chest!" London urged, continuing to smirk.

"Naw London, I don't want to bore you with me and O.T.'s problems. I'll just have to deal with him and that black spook Chocolate Bunny on my own."

"It's all right, Paris. We're friends, aren't we?"

"Yeah girl, but I'm gonna just sit here and think. Thanks, though."

London was disappointed that Paris choose not to confide in her, but she wasn't going to let that stop the fake compassion from pouring. She wanted O.T., thug or not, Paris's man or not—fuck Chocolate Bunny, Santa Claus, and the Tooth Fairy! They were all irrelevant to her!

If Gran was watching down from heaven, she would be ashamed at how London was behaving. Yet, London felt like the world had stepped on her for the last time. From day one she always tried doing the right thing and the only reward she got in return were several swift, hard kicks in the ass. Life for London was not fair in her eyes.

Her parents were both murdered when she was a baby. Gran was gone, the only one who truly loved her. Her favorite uncle, Stone, was killed. Her virginity was taken from her against her will. She had to suddenly drop out of school and now the only thing or person who she had left to cling to, Kenya, was slowly being snatched away by these strangers that her twin now called family. It was no way that London intended on that happening, no matter what the cost. Her vindictive alter ego had taken over and she didn't care who paid the price for her happiness.

What's taking them so long up there? London thought, staring at the stairs. *I hope that O.T. is okay. Maybe he needs me?*

Kenya had only gotten around to removing Storm's filthy, sweat-soaked shirt by cutting it off, when she noticed a huge-sized dirty gauze taped across his shoulder. She peeled it back. It revealed an ugly, open sore.

"O.T., my God, come here! What is this? What happened?"

The doctor ran over and investigated. "It looks like a gunshot wound to me. As far as I can tell, I think the bullet went in and out. I need to get a closer look at him. Hurry and flip him on his side."

O.T. did as he was instructed, gently handling his older brother. He held him in his arms just as their mother used to do when they were kids before she started smoking. Big Doc B rubbed his hands over Storm's back.

"Yes, here it is! Here's the exit wound. Yeah, I was right, it was a clear gunshot, in and out," he verified his earlier prediction. "And it appears as if it has been treated with bacterial ointment of some sort. There are no signs of infections. Someone seems to have cleaned it up pretty good."

"What the hell does that mean? Is he okay?" Kenya worried, confused. "Shouldn't we take him to the hospital?"

"We can't," O.T. cut her off. "That shit is out— no hospital!"

"Yes, Kenya, I'm afraid he's right, we can't risk doing that. You see, the doctors are sworn by law to contact the authorities when treating any gunshot wounds big or small," Big Doc B reasoned with her. "Besides, like I said, all in all, he's okay and healing just fine. Just let nature take its course. In the meantime, I'm gonna give you some morphine to keep him sedated and still. If he awakes in pain keep him calm and up the dosage slightly. I can also give you penicillin to fight off any of the remaining infections."

"How is he gonna eat?" Kenya inquired, having no idea how to care for Storm. "Or pee?"

"When he awakes, even for a few seconds, feed him warm broth, even if you pour a little bit down his throat, but the other part is on you. I sure hope that you're up to playing nursemaid for a couple of weeks. Storm's gonna need it!"

Kenya glanced back at Storm, who was tossing and turning and seemed to be gasping for air. The doctor had O.T. go out to his car and bring in a big, sealed cardboard box. After they got Storm comfortable in the bed, Big Doc B opened the box and pulled out ointments, syringes, penicillin, and plenty of morphine. He instructed Kenya in all the aspects of being the perfect caregiver to the badly injured Storm.

Storm was finally resting peacefully, back at home, in his own bed. With an IV in his arm, a slow-drip morphine keeping him doped up, and all his wounds treated, the doctor was finished for the night. O.T. escorted Big Doc B out to his car and paid him a nice chunk of change for the long, extended house visit and his agreed-upon silence.

Kenya stayed next to Storm's bedside, rubbing his forehead and begging for his forgiveness. Paris fixed some tea for them both and made her way upstairs also, deciding to spend the night and lend her best friend some much-needed moral support. That left O.T. and London all alone in a dimly-lit living room.

"Is she okay up there?" London whined, leaning her head on O.T. "You think Kenya needs me?" London would be first in line to receive an Academy Award for her acting performance, knowing in all reality she was starting to care less about Kenya's feelings.

"Naw, but I think I might need your ass. How about that?" O.T. had a long, rough day. Seeing his big brother and hero broken down had taken a heavy toll on him. "Come to think of it, I do need you."

O.T. rested his head in London's lap and in no time flat he was snoring, not once giving a second thought to Paris being in the same house. His brother was home and nothing else seemed to matter.

Things are about to be in my favor for once! O.T. said he needed me! Not Paris's stuck-up-ass and not that slut-bag Chocolate Bunny they keep arguing about, but me! London couldn't help but smile as she closed her eyes, finally dozing off to sleep herself.

Hopefully to avoid conflict, Paris and Kenya were upstairs doing the same. They had all had enough drama for the day and Paris catching her man cheating with her best friend's twin sister would only make the day end with a bang. No doubt about it, it was going to be a long couple of weeks for Kenya, Storm, Paris, O.T., and London.

12

Da Game Ain't Fair

Several days passed and Storm was basically still out of his rabbit-ass mind. There was little to no change in his overall condition. The swelling in his jaw was, however, going down, but still had some very bad bruising. The gunshot wound was the only thing that appeared to heal quickly. Storm would move his bad leg from time to time in his sleep, when he would scream out in pain, like he was a small animal being hunted down, caught, and killed. Watching him in that state made a weary Kenya cry on the regular at his bedside.

The perfect brush waves Storm always sported were gone. His hair was growing daily and nappy as a fuck. His beard was thick and looked downright messy as hell. And even though Kenya kept his face washed, his once-brown, perfectly toned skin was dry and blemished. With all the weight that he had dropped since Javier first held him hostage, Storm was only a shadow of the man that he used to be. He stayed unconscious most of the time because of the intense pain he was suffering, making Kenya's job of getting even a tiny sip of soup down his throat almost an impossible task.

And then it was keeping the covers dry and clean, which was a bitch, seeing how Storm was pissing on himself and sweating like a motherfucker. Kenya refused to use the Depend undergarments that Big Doc B suggested. She felt like that was humiliating for her fiancé to have to deal with when he did come back to reality. When he would awaken, all Storm would do was moan and mumble about a lot of nothing that made no sense. Each day seemed to stretch out longer and longer before he would fully recover to his old self and things got back to normal. Kenya was exhausted, but was extremely devoted.

Big Doc B stopped by every other day to examine Storm and check on his healing process. Slowly, he was decreasing the amount of morphine that Storm was under the influence of. He didn't want to keep him sedated so long that he wasn't able to regain use of his leg without the aid of therapy. Big Doc B knew that with some of the excruciating pain, Storm would have to be a thoroughbred trooper and man the fuck up. It would be some hard shit to do, but nothing that Storm couldn't handle.

KENYA

"I don't know how much more of this I can take." Kenya was distraught and moving around like a zombie. Staying up late at night, waiting and catering to Storm's every need was breaking her down both physically and mentally. She was starting to truly look like hot death on a stick. It had been days since she had a long, hot bath or sat down to watch her stories on television. Her hair was standing on the top of her head and her face had forgotten what makeup was. Every moment that Kenya was awake, she spent posted by Storm just in case he opened his eyes and needed any little thing.

London would help her at times, but felt like it wasn't her duty or her responsibility to be a stranger's slave. Only when O.T. was around would she put on a front and act like she gave a shit about Kenya or Storm. Kenya had just finished changing the sheets and getting Storm settled when she heard her cell phone ring. She kissed Storm on his dry lips and went into the den to answer the call.

"Hello?"

"Hey, Kenya! What's good, woman?"

"Who is this?" Kenya yawned, sitting back on the couch, laying her head back on the arm.

"Oh, it's like that? Your ass out in Dallas and forgot about me and your godson that quick!"

"Oh, my God! Young Foy, is that you? It's so good to hear your voice!"

"Yeah, it's me. I was just checking in with you and wanted to give your sexy self some good news."

"I need some good news right about now. I hope that it's about Jaylin. Does he miss his Auntie Kenya?"

"You know he misses you, but that ain't the news."

"What is it, boy! Stop playing with me!" Kenya managed to crack a smile for the first time in weeks.

"My CD just hit the shelves! That's what's really good!" Young Foy was excited and Kenya could feel his energy jump through the phone. "Me and Jaylin is gonna be rich. My shit is about to blow the fuck up."

"Damn, I'm so happy for you. I knew you could do that shit. I always told you that you had mad skills."

"Yeah, you always did encourage a brother and help me get on my feet."

"Right, right!" Kenya said, smiling.

"That's why you the first person that I called. I got love for you Kenya, flat out."

"I got love for you too. My girl Raven is probably up in heaven dancing on the clouds with pride."

"Yeah, I miss the shit outta her ass. Jaylin is starting to look more and more like his mama every single day that passes." Young Foy glanced over at his sleeping stepson and smiled. "I'm about to head to the cemetery in a few and take some fresh flowers. I feel close to her when I'm there."

"Next time I'm back in Detroit, I'm gonna have to go out there." Kenya rested her eyes, momentarily reminiscing about the good old days when her and Raven were hustlin' hard, making all the cheddar in Heads Up.

"Me and Jaylin both will be glad to see you."

Before the conversation ended, Kenya's call waiting clicked in with another call. It was from Paris and O.T.'s crib and she had to take it.

"Hey, that's my other line. I'm gonna call you back later on tonight and give Jaylin a huge hug and kiss from me."

"Okay, Kenya! I'll holler!"

Young Foy hung up and Kenya answered the other line. "Hello?"

PARIS

"Why every day it gotta be the same old fake shit from you, O.T.?" Paris was in the bathroom, yelling at O.T. as he took his morning shower. "You just got in this motherfucker at four-thirty in the morning, now you back out the door again! Nigga, I ain't slow or crazy. Ain't shit open that late at night, but the jailhouse and a stankin' bitch's pussy."

O.T. continued to let the hot water pound his body as he zoned Paris completely out of his mind. His hands rubbed the soap on his chest and let his imagination drift to thoughts of fucking the shit out of London. He had his fingers up inside of her tight, moist pussy and had sucked on her titties, but had never actually given her the dick. His thick, long manhood throbbed from his hands letting the lather work its way up and down as he stroked it hard. At that second O.T. would have spit in his dead great-grandmother's face if he could have had London bent over with his dick knee-deep up in her. He loved Paris as much as a man could love a woman, but her constant nagging was starting to turn him off. His motto was that there was nothing better than brand-new pussy. And London was his new target.

"Do you hear me talking to your half-nickel slick dumb ass?" Paris yanked back the shower curtain and rolled her eyes, immediately catching a serious attitude. "I'm trying to talk to you and you in here beating your motherfucking meat! You ain't shit!"

"Why don't you get out of my ear with all that ying-yanging and put your mouth to better use?" O.T.'s shit was about ready to explode, with or without Paris's help with it. "Now come on, girl. Come catch some of this cream!"

"Nigga, please. Why don't you get that bitch you was with last night to suck your little dick? That broken-ass cell phone of yours called me back after you hung up and I heard them bitches giggling and shit."

"Damn, Paris, stop tripping and come get on your knees!" O.T. let what his woman said come in one ear and fly out the other. "You know ain't shit little about this motherfucking monster I got in my hands! So why don't you come see Daddy?"

Paris was pissed off even more by O.T. ignoring the information she'd just confronted him with. "Didn't you hear what I said, with your trick-ass? I heard that slut talking about the ringer on her phone being 'Gold Digger'!" Paris pulled her robe tight and folded her arms. "What kind of real woman would have that bullshit on their phone? Don't fuck around and give me AIDS or something! You're a poor excuse for a man!"

O.T. had enough of her accusations and insults. This time he was innocent and didn't feel like all that drama she was bringing his way. O.T. was past running late for an appointment and still had to swing by a couple of his dope spots before he headed for his meeting. He was determined to get his nuts out the sand before he left and snatched an angry Paris into the shower with him.

Her hair was now drenched and her short, pink robe was soaking wet, causing her nipples to harden. In the middle of her struggling to break free from him, O.T.'s dick got harder than it ever had been before. He quickly turned her around, pressing her face on the wet shower wall, raising up her robe. He ran his hands down the crack of her ass and soon he had his index finger working her out. Paris was out of breath and gave in to her man as the steam filled the bathroom. He shoved all eight and a half inches up into her while he watched the water drip on her backside. Right before he was about to cum, O.T. shut his eyes, imagining that she was London. He tilted his head back and almost busted for what seemed like an hour straight past eternity.

"Now! Do that seem like a nigga been fucking around on your silly-ass?" O.T. blew Paris a kiss as he stepped out the shower, grabbing a towel to dry off. He splashed on some Armani Black

Code and started getting dressed. Rubbing lotion on his face and brushing his hair, he double-checked the mirror twice, clipped his cell phone on his jeans, and got his wallet out of the nightstand. "I love you, Paris!"

Paris was too exhausted from the sexual beat-down that he had just put on her to even argue. "Whatever!"

"Here's some dollars for you to go get your wig tightened up for Daddy! And buy a new outfit." O.T. peeled off four or five hundreds and tossed them on the dresser before he left out the door.

"I need to talk to you," Paris yelled out, still weak in the knees. "I'm serious!

"I'll be back later, boo! Keep it hot for a nigga!"

Paris was left speechless as she heard him pull out of the parking lot and away from the apartment. "I know that bastard is cheating on me!" She had to vent and decided to call her girl. Maybe she could convince her to go to the hair salon with her. After grabbing the cordless phone, she dialed Kenya's cell and waited for her to pick up.

GIRLFRIENDS

"Hey, Kenya. Are you busy?"

"Naw chick, not really. I was just taking a little break and just got off the phone with an old friend. What's really good with you?"

"Girl, I'm sitting over here mad as a son of a bitch. If I didn't have a lot of self-control, I think I would just put two bullets in O.T.'s cheating-ass and get it over with!" Paris stood in front of the mirror, brushing her wet hair back into a ponytail.

"Slow down, Paris." Kenya knew that her best friend was in pain and mentally tired of O.T. and his crap.

"Naw girl, enough is enough. I done about had it with him and his dogmatic ways!"

"Paris. You ain't making any sense right now. Tell me exactly what went on over there."

"First that fool had the nerve to slither his behind in the house at damn near four-thirty this morning," she argued as her friend listened. "Even when I close the club at night that nigga will bug out if I'm more than five minutes late getting home, but he thinks he can fall up in the crib whenever! Girl, bye with all that—for real!"

"Dang! Where did he say he was? Or did he?" Kenya shook her head with disgust, knowing when it came to Storm's brother he could've been anywhere with anybody.

"You know that bullshit would be too much-like, right, but that ain't even the bad part!" Paris threw herself on the bed and put her feet up on the headboard. "His cell phone dialed me back by mistake and I swear to God I heard that tack-head Chocolate Bunny running her big mouth in the background."

"You lying to me!" Kenya was now also frustrated about the shit. "Please tell me you lying, Paris!"

"Hmph, I wish the fuck I was. And when I asked the two-timing dog he started playing the dumb role, then he had the audacity to flip the script and take the damn pussy!" Paris was shouting into the phone receiver by this time and was back on her feet. "If I didn't have an allergy to fucking prison, I'd kill him in his fucking sleep!"

Kenya couldn't understand why O.T. couldn't be loyal to one woman and was so damn ruthless. He was a bona fide ho! If she was dealing with a Negro like that, it would be no way that she would tolerate all the mess that Paris put up with. Paris was a way better woman than she was.

O.T. would stop by the condo every afternoon and sit by Storm. He filled him in on all the news from the club and the goings-on in the streets. The fact that Storm was doped up on morphine and didn't even realize that O.T. was in the room, never once stopped his brother from talking. O.T. had a split personality. He was like Dr. Jekyll and Mr. Hyde. He was sweet as pie one minute and the next, a beast ready to kill you at the drop of a dime.

"Kenya, I ain't lying. That boy gonna end up in a casket one day double-crossing a bitch like me!" Paris knocked a framed picture of him and her to the floor. "He got me twisted! Shit, I need a damn drink!"

"Girl, why don't you come on over so we can kick it in person? I can get London to cook us up some hot wings and fries," Kenya suggested, wanting some company other than Storm and her sister, both of whom were quiet.

Paris looked at herself again in the mirror, coming up with a better idea. "Why don't I just swing by and swoop your ass up? We can hit the Steak House, then the hair salon. How about it?"

"Girl, you know I can't leave Storm alone. He needs someone by his side constantly."

"You need to get out and get some fresh air. Your sister can stay home and look after him," Paris pleaded with her best friend. "I know you look a hot mess right about now."

Kenya noticed that three of her fingernails were in bad need of a fill-in and her polish was chipped. She then tried running her fingers through her hair, but was stopped by a few naps. "Yeah, I do need a touch-up and a manicure."

"Then it's settled. Let me get dressed and I'll come get you!" Paris was geeked to finally, even if it was temporary, have her road dawg back.

"Pump your brakes, Paris. I gotta go ask London first."

"Okay cool, but hurry up and call me back before I jump in the shower and wash O.T.'s good lying-ass off me."

"You silly as hell," Kenya giggled. "Just give me a minute to check and see what's up."

Paris and Kenya automatically assumed that London would be the perfect person to stay with Storm, considering the fact she didn't have a life of her own. Kenya's life and world had somehow swallowed it whole. The best friends never thought maybe London wanted to go out for lunch or get her hair done. She was also stuck in the house in a strange town with no friends. But that didn't stop Kenya from asking her for a favor just the same.

Kenya stopped in to check on Storm before going downstairs. He was quiet and seemed to be resting peacefully. Since the dosage was decreasing, he seemed to be in and out of consciousness more often. She kissed him softly and made her way to the lower level of the condo. When she got in the living room, she found her twin sister doing something that she'd never seen her do before. London was stretched out across the couch, feet up on a pillow, watching rap videos and even acting like she was enjoying them.

"No, you ain't! I thought you said videos were stupid and degrading to women? Now your butt sitting up here posted like a motherfucker!"

"Shut up!" London threw a pillow at Kenya. "I'm just looking at this ghetto trash, trying to understand exactly what everyone finds so interesting."

London was a lie and the truth wasn't in her. She had been keeping her eyes glued on the way the girls danced and moved their asses, to the way they dressed. She understood why O.T. liked Paris, who was smart, pretty, and always had his back. Paris truly had her shit together; that part was undeniable. Even if she wanted to hate, she couldn't find much. But that serpent Chocolate Bunny was altogether different. From what London had heard about her, she was no more than a dirty, unkempt gutter rat. Whatever O.T. saw in her, Paris, Kenya, and London were all hard-pressed to realize. Maybe all the wild, nasty videos would shed some light on the dilemma and help London to turn O.T. on. If it took being sleazy and a little hot in the ass to achieve the ultimate goal of having O.T. all to herself, then so be it, that's what she'd do.

"Listen, London, would you mind sitting upstairs with Storm for a few hours so I can run out for a little while with Paris? Please?"

London had been hoping and wishing that Kenya would leave the house so that she could be alone with O.T. when he would come over for one of his daily afternoon visits. Now was her time and to make shit even better, Kenya was hanging out with Paris. She would have O.T. all to herself.

"Yeah, sis, I'll stay here. No problem."

Kenya went and called Paris back, informing her that their plan was a go. She took a quick bath and got dressed. Meanwhile, London stayed downstairs and plotted her seduction game plan. Twenty minutes later Paris pulled up, blowing her horn.

"Don't worry about Storm. I'll make sure to check in on him every fifteen minutes and give him his medicine on time," London convinced her sister all would be well. "Go and have a nice time. He's in good hands. Take all the time you need."

"Say you promise!" Kenya hugged London.

"Yeah, I promise!" London walked her twin to the front porch, waving hello to Paris, knowing she was secretly scheming on stealing her man right from underneath her nose.

13

Fuck Da World

O.T.

O.T. had the sounds in his car on bump as usual, causing all the other car windows to vibrate that he passed along the way. The long valet line at the mall's main entrance didn't matter one bit to him as he pulled up to the front and parked his ride up on the curb. He and his brother not only knew the parking attendants, they hung out with the lot's owners on a regular basis, making O.T. feel like he was above waiting for shit. He threw the guy his keys in case of emergency and walked inside.

He was already ten minutes late and wasted no time in going over to the designated meeting spot near the food court. It was always busy with people moving about, so he and his visitor would more than likely go unnoticed. It was no way that he wanted to draw attention to them. He looked around and didn't see the person yet, so he decided to order a large soda. By the time he reached in his pocket to pay the cashier for it, she was there.

"Hey babe, did you get me something wet to put in my mouth?" she flirted while sticking out her tongue to reveal the small gold ball pierced through the middle.

"Damn girl! You slick with your shit. I didn't even see your ass coming." O.T. ordered her a small soda to drink and fought the urge for her to lick the head of his dick just like she used to. "A brother better be careful dealing with your good creeping ass!"

"You know how I do, baby. Ain't shit changed since back in the day!" She sipped her drink slowly out the straw as she stared into O.T.'s eyes.

"I heard that," He took a large gulp of the soda and tossed the rest of it into one of the garbage cans. "But I'm trying to take care of some other shit today so I need to hurry the fuck up!"

O.T. took his time as he scanned his surroundings for signs of any trouble or unwelcome eyes on them. When he felt the coast was clear he pulled out a gigantic knot of money, big enough to choke King Kong, and slipped it casually into Nicole's oversized purse.

"Do I need to count it?" she playfully teased, pushing his arm. "Or can I trust you?"

"Come on, girl, act like you know! I don't make moves that ain't right or have you forgotten?" O.T.'s eyes shot down toward the huge print in his pants. "I'll expect to hear from your smart-ass tonight!"

"Yeah, yeah, yeah, I'll see you later at the club, don't worry." Nicole grinned, closing her purse. Being the true whore she was, she stood up, straightening out the ultra-short bright red sundress that was plastered to her thick frame.

"That's a bet, and be on time!" O.T. winked, getting a quick, glimpse of her two firm breasts, which were close to almost falling out of her clothes.

"Damn, I almost forgot. Can you keep a secret?" She put one hand on her hip and the other in his face.

"What is it?" He waited for her to answer.

Nicole leaned up and whispered in O.T.'s ear, causing him to smile. He then hugged her tightly and kissed her on her forehead before they parted ways.

"Okay, then drinks on me later," O.T. laughed as he walked away to the valet. "Or something like that, I guess!"

"You crazy boy!"

"Ain't that some foul-ass shit?"

Paris's homegirl and spy down at Alley Cats, Jordan, happened to be at the mall at the right time. She was busy spending the money that she made from doing a private party the night before and fucked around and got an eyeful of what was sure to be labeled the gossip of the year. Paris's man O.T. was giving Nicole Daniels a gang of loot. After all the denying that he was doing to Paris about that tramp, he was out in public, in the middle of the freaking food court no less, tearing the bitch off proper style and to top it all, hugging her black-ass.

"Hell naw! I've gotta call Paris!" Jordan smirked as she whipped out her cell to put O.T.'s ass straight on blast. *It's gonna be a whole lot of crazy shit jumping off at Alley Cats tonight,* Jordan thought to herself as Paris's voice mail clicked on. She left her a message, "Hey girl, this is Jordan. Hit me back as soon as you get this. I need to put a bug in your ear about a little something. Trust me, you're gonna bug all the way when I tell you what I just seen. Call me back first thing first!"

GIRLFRIENDS

"Kenya, I'm so happy that you came out to hang with me." Paris had the air-conditioning on high and a mix CD pumping. "I miss your wild ass!"

"Child, me too. Now you know I love Storm like a motherfucker, but a bitch did need some air. Plus, look at my nails and please, let's not even mention this tangled mess on my head! I walked passed the mirror this morning and scared the hell out of myself."

Paris and Kenya couldn't help but laugh until tears came out their eyes. It was just like old times.

"What about this crap?" Paris snatched one of O.T.'s baseball caps off her head. "If that nasty fool nigga wasn't so busy trying to take that pussy, my shit wouldn't be on the nut."

They had just finished up with a good lunch and a couple of strong drinks and were on their way to the hair salon. Hair In Da Hood was the most popular spot in all of Dallas when it came to getting your hair looking top-notch. It stayed packed with wall-to-wall customers who would often range from lawyers and doctors to freaks and hoes.

Charday was the salon owner and the main stylist that everyone wanted to do their hair. Her chair stayed full. Most of the time a person would have to make an appointment at least two or three weeks ahead of time. But of course, Ms. Charday, a true hustler, would always make exceptions for her special clients and her good friends. And since Paris and Kenya were known for being big-ass spenders when it came to tipping, they automatically fit into both categories.

Her man played professional ball and bought Hair In Da Hood as a birthday present for her twenty-first birthday. After some major remodeling, a few hair shows, and a gang of slamming commercials, Charday was off and running in the hair game, clocking major figures. Nine out of ten times, even if you got there early, you'd end up leaving late.

In between the bootleg-movie guys hustling, the supposed-to-be-authentic purse dude or somebody's grandmother selling soul food dinners, not to mention all the off-the-wall gossip that would fly in, out, and around the salon, it could very easily turn into an all-day event. Some of the nosy bitches around town would live for the weekends so they could get into the next hoe's mix and cause trouble.

Nevertheless, Paris and Kenya were on a mission to pamper themselves for the day and that meant no stress and no drama or trauma.

"I've got a good idea. For the rest of the afternoon, let's make a pact not to bring up, mention, whine or complain about that pair of brothers we're linked up with." Paris stuck her hand out and waited. "Well, you gonna leave me hanging or what?"

"Naw chick, I got you!" Kenya gave her a play. "Bet it up for real!"

"Now that's what the fuck I'm talking about!" Paris yelled out as she adjusted the volume up as high as it could go.

The girls put their seats back as they floated down the highway toward the salon. Fifteen minutes later they were pulling up in a crowded parking lot, trying to find a space that wasn't eight doors down or around the corner.

"Damn! Is every trick in town up in that joint?" Paris frowned as she pulled her car into a tiny corner of the lot. "I hope our girl ain't too booked. I'd hate to have to smack somebody out the chair, but my shit is on emergency status." Paris looked at Kenya with a straight face like she was serious.

She turned the car's ignition off and reached for her purse that was on the backseat before she made her exit.

"Dang, you right, Paris." Kenya joined in on talking shit as she got out of the car. "Charday and them must be giving away free cheese, honey, and butter inside. I ain't never seen this motherfucker on bump like this either."

The girls swung the door open and stepped inside. Just as they figured, the salon was packed. Sable was the receptionist and was standing behind the desk, trying her best to reason with one of the many irate customers who were getting tired of waiting.

"Hey y'all!" Sable happily waved her hand in the air. "Long time, no see. Where y'all divas been hiding?"

"Just chillin' a little bit, that's all," Kenya replied.

"Yeah, Sable, we call our self letting our hair have a break from all the chemicals," Paris added, trying to play off their recent absence from the scene.

"I heard that," Sable responded, seeming frustrated at the phone that was ringing non-stop and the angry woman with conditioner in her damp hair in a plastic cap who kept coming back up to the desk to complain.

Kenya took a quick survey of the waiting room and asked the million-dollar question. "Hey Sable, how many customers do Charday have backed up in this tiny motherfucker and can she squeeze us in?"

"Well, let me check the book. I'm sure she can definitely work something out for y'all two." Sable grabbed the sign-in sheet and took the pencil out from behind her ear.

The lady who was standing there was pissed and sucked her teeth as she waited for Sable's answer. She had been there ever since 11:45 in the morning and still hadn't been rinsed or blow-dried. Same old story, once again as always, Charday had overbooked and had folks pissed.

"I'm gonna go speak to Charday myself and make sure." Kenya stopped Sable from trying to rearrange things. "I'll be right back."

Paris twisted her lip up at the agitated lady and let out a loud sigh. "Go ahead, girl, and see what's popping. I'll wait here and keep Ms. Thang and Sable company."

The woman took that as her cue to go back to her seat, shut the fuck up, and wait until she was called. It was either that or nine out of ten times get a quick double-trouble-ass beat-down from Kenya and Paris. When Kenya returned she had good news and bad news. The good news was that Charday could fit them both in, but they had to give her at least thirty minutes to finish up with the girl in her chair. The bad news was that she had to slip Charday a crisp hundred-dollar bill and promised her a bottle of new perfume for the deed. It was all part of being Storm and O.T.'s girls. They had to play the role—after all, no matter where they went, bitches hated. It came along with the territory being labeled "the shit."

Paris and Kenya sat down next to the angry woman who had pulled out a book and was totally engulfed in reading. She appeared not to even care anymore that she was still waiting as she turned page after page without once looking up.

Paris opened her purse and got out her cell phone to look at the time. "Shit, I didn't hear this thing ringing." The screen said *two missed calls* and had a small envelope in the upper corner indicating that someone had left a voice message. Paris stepped into the bathroom to listen to the message. It was much quieter in there. It was no women gossiping and the sound of the loud radio and television was muffled. *Jordan wants me to call her as soon as possible. What the fuck could this be about?* Paris wondered as she returned the call. On the first ring, Jordan picked up.

"Hey Paris, what took you so long?"

"Hey sis, I had my phone in my purse, what's the deal?"

"Girl, before I tell you this bullshit, you'd better sit down first."

"You too silly! Stop tripping and tell me what you gotsta say! What's going on?"

"Well girl, I was just out at the mall jacking off some spare change and guess who the fuck I saw?"

"Who?" Paris's heart started pumping fast as she awaited the answer from Jordan. From the tone of Jordan's voice, Paris could tell that the name that was sure to come out of her mouth would bring automatic fury.

"I seen that slut ho Nicole."

"Nicole! Who the fuck is Nicole?" Paris tried to keep her now-agitated voice down.

"Come on, Paris, you know who I'm talking about, girl . . . Chocolate damn Bunny, that's fucking Nicole!"

"And? What's the big deal about that? Hoes gotta shop too!" Paris tried to crack a joke to ease the pain of what might be coming next.

Jordan didn't laugh as she gave her homegirl the lowdown. "Yeah, but she wasn't alone. She was at the food court all hugged up with O.T."

"What! What you say?" Paris closed her eyes, wishing she hadn't just heard what she thought she heard. "Are you for sure?"

"Yes Paris, I'm certain," Jordan reassured her of what she had just witnessed. "He was wearing some dark-colored jeans, a Mavericks jersey, and Tims. That trick Chocolate Bunny had on a skintight red dress and was rocking a big Gucci bag. Knowing her fake-ass, it was probably bootleg!" Jordan vindictively added.

"It's all good in the hood. I'm gonna handle it." Paris pretended to be brave as her hand shook. "I got this!"

"Oh, yeah it's more. I even saw him give that tramp a nice-sized knot of cash! Hell, I wanted to follow that tack-head and rob her my damn self! With her stankin' no-good low-down dirty-ass! She ain't shit!"

"All right, Jordan, good looking on the info. I'll see you later tonight at the club."

Paris was heated as well as devastated. She went inside of one of the stalls and shut the door. When the tears started to flow she didn't want any of the women in the salon to see her at one of her weakest moments. After ten minutes of having an emotional fit, she splashed cold water on her face and went to fill Kenya in on the latest.

"What took you so long in there?" Kenya inquired. "I was about to send in a search party!"

"I was on the phone."

"Talking to who? And why are your eyes all red and shit? Have you been crying?"

Paris pulled her baseball cap down over her face in an attempt to shield any nosy bitches from noticing the same thing that Kenya had. "I called Jordan back. She left me an urgent message."

"Jordan from the club? What kind of message? Is everything going all right down at Alley Cats?" Kenya hoped that shit was in order. She didn't have the time or strength to go to the club and straighten out a damn thang.

Paris was agitated, trying her best whisper. "It ain't the club. It's O.T.'s no-good ass. Jordan just seen him at the fucking mall."

"What's wrong with that?"

"He was there with Chocolate Bunny." Paris felt like she had just been socked in the stomach as soon as the words passed her lips. "All up on that bitch—caking!"

Kenya was almost speechless. "Is she sure? You know how females like to start rumors—hatin'."

"Naw girl, she knew exactly what that cheating Negro was wearing from foot to fro." Paris sniffed, fighting back the tears. "The worst part is his ass is serving that black bitch up like a queen. Jordan said he gave Chocolate Bunny some dough like she was wifey or something."

"That trifling nigga must be smoking crack!" Kenya said with her hand on Paris's shoulder. "Something ain't right! O.T. and her?"

Less than ten minutes had passed in between the time that the best friends tried to figure out what was wrong with O.T.'s simple behind for doing that dumb shit to Paris and the five seconds it took Chocolate Bunny to prance her slap-happy-ass through the front door of the salon. She was dressed just the way that Jordan described over the phone—all the way down to her purse she was sporting, which, by the way, was definitely without doubt bootleg.

She proudly marched up to the reception desk like she owned stock in the bitch. "Yeah, I need Charday to tighten up my weave real quick!"

"I'm sorry, Nicole, but she's all booked up for the rest of today." Sable chewed her bubble gum and gave her a funny look. "What about tomorrow? She has a ten o'clock open."

Chocolate Bunny reached in her handbag and started flashing money. "Well, I'll pay a hundred dollars to any of y'all customers that wanna give up y'all spot with Charday!"

While she was showboating, Kenya was trying everything in her power to keep Paris in her seat.

"No, that bird ain't up in here spending my money. I outta go over there and knock her ass out!" Paris was fuming. "I hate the fuck out of her!"

"Listen, Paris, it is what it is! Don't let that girl or any other of these females up in here catch you off your square! Boss up—do you hear me?" Kenya was in Paris's ear, being the voice of reason. "Now come on and let's just jet before you embarrass yourself. We can deal with her later. Besides, you should at least give O.T. a chance to explain before you mess around and hurt somebody. Go out to the car and call him!"

Gathering her composure, Paris finally agreed. When the pair was almost out of the door, Chocolate Bunny spotted them and decided to do what she did best, make a scene and overplay her position.

"Oh, hey ladies! I didn't see y'all sitting over there. You two could have spoken or something." She was being bogus as a three-dollar bill. She knew that it wasn't no love shared between them. The only thing that they had up to this point in common was Alley Cats.

"Hey girl," Kenya said, nodding. "We kinda in a rush, so . . ."

"Okay, then damn, don't let me stop you," Chocolate Bunny giggled, rolling her neck. "Or you either, Miss Paris!"

Paris couldn't take it any longer. Her temper was on boiling status. "Listen up, bitch, don't even speak to my fine-ass! A ho like you ain't even in my damn league, okay! Now carry your messy behind the fuck on, before I give your family some arrangements to make for you!"

"Hold tight, Paris! Who you calling bitch, bitch! Is you insane or something?" Chocolate Bunny sucked her teeth, looking Paris up and down like it could and would be whatever. "And don't be threatening me either, Paris, I don't like that kinda shit! Me or my man!"

"Your man?" Paris flared up even more.

"You heard me! I said my man, ho—mine!" she repeated with certainty.

"Yeah, right! You got me all fucked up! I don't make threats, I make promises!" Paris pointed her finger in her face. "Fuck you and him! Believe that!"

Kenya stepped in the middle before either one got a chance to swing. The entire salon was staring at the group, waiting for a show. Charday, being the peacemaker, came over and asked them to calm down or leave. They were all good clients, but business was business and they were all tripping. The last thing she wanted or needed in her salon was a knock-down, drag-out.

Before Paris and Kenya could oblige to Charday's wishes and get out the salon door good, they heard the song "Gold Digger" playing. It was the ring tone that was on Chocolate Bunny's cell phone. Hearing that tune, Paris zoned out, having an instantaneous flashback to the other night when O.T.'s phone dialed her back and recklessly sucker punched the female in her jaw, causing her to fall to the floor smack down on her ass and at the feet of waiting clients.

"She was past due on that one!" Paris snickered as her and Kenya finally got in the car and pulled off.

Damn! Kenya thought as she drove away. *Alley Cats is gonna be on the nut tonight when Nicole gets there. I really gotsa go to the club now!*

14

How, What, Why

O.T.

Driving down the interstate with the warm air blowing on his face, O.T. let the music take control of his mind. He was once again lost in thoughts of London's perfectly shaped ass. He secretly always wanted to fuck the shit out of Kenya, but considering the fact that she was Storm's woman, that made her off limits. Seeing how London was her identical twin, she was the next best thing to actually sticking the dick to his brother's girl. In his twisted mindset it would be like hittin' them both off at the same time.

As O.T. felt his hard pipe pulsate through his jeans, he smiled seeing his exit and quickly made the turn. It was now only a couple of short blocks to get to his brother's crib for his daily visit. His dick was stiff as a board. If he played his cards right, O.T. hoped he might get a few minutes alone with London, at least to feel on her titties or grab a handful of her ass. No matter what he did, she was with it.

Kenya always did her best to cock-block him when it came to her sister, letting him know that it was no way that she was being a part of any backstabbing conspiracy plotted against Paris. If London was in a room with O.T., you betta best believe that Kenya was in that bitch too. Day after day Kenya informed him that there wasn't a damn thing going down on her watch. Little did Kenya or O.T. have any idea that today would be his lucky day.

LONDON

No sooner than Kenya and Paris bent the corner, London ran back in the house and straight up the stairs. She tiptoed into her sister's room, past a sleeping Storm, and went into the closet. It was now time to select an outfit that would make O.T. lose his mind when he saw her. For days, she had taken notes from the videos and knew that with Kenya out of the house, she might finally have the chance to put her plan in effect. After snatching a short blue jean miniskirt off the hanger and a powder-blue T-shirt that was sure to fit tight, London headed for the shower.

She used some of her sister's favorite cucumber melon body wash as she felt the warm water hit her nude body. London then rubbed in plenty of the matching lotion after drying off. Slipping on Kenya's new shell-covered sandals, she pranced downstairs. She then admired her work in the mirror. London now looked exactly just like Kenya. Her once dull appearance was gone and the bait was now set for O.T. to get trapped.

I know that he's gonna want me now! If this doesn't entice him, I don't know what will, she thought as she hugged herself. *I just hope that he gets here at the usual time and Kenya stays gone. I don't need any obstacles getting in my way!* London went into the kitchen, getting one of Kenya's peach-flavored wine coolers out of the refrigerator. She hated the way that they tasted, but holding the bottle in her hand made her feel more mature and sexy. Plus, most of the females in the nasty uncut videos all had glasses in their hands as they danced around.

Where is he at? she wondered, watching the clock. Sitting down on the couch, crossing her legs, London held the remote in her right hand, clicking channels while tapping the cooler bottle with the left.

***

O.T. pulled into the driveway and turned off his car. He sat back in the custom leather bucket seats, leaning his neck on the headrest. O.T. had to collect his thoughts and closed his eyes briefly. Seeing his brother still suffering after all this time was causing him to have constant migraine headaches. As much as he tried being the strong person that all the people involved depended on, he was starting to crack from the heavy, stressed-filled pressure. When he sat up, opening up his eyes, O.T. saw Kenya standing in the doorway waving to him.

"Damn, I guess I should go ahead and go in," he mumbled as he unlocked the car door. Getting closer up toward the door, he busted out laughing. "Oh shit, tell me I'm seeing thangs!" O.T. stopped in his tracks, folding his arms and started shaking his head. The jersey he was wearing showed off every muscle, his jeans sagged perfectly, and his Tims had the tongue stuck out with the laces loose.

"What's so funny?" London asked with her hands firmly on her hips. She had done her best to imitate Kenya and now O.T. was standing there laughing in her face. "What's wrong? You don't like it?" London stood still as she waited for him to speak.

"Ain't shit funny, ma. Ain't shit funny at all." He rubbed his chin, licking his lips. "I just thought that you was Kenya and shit. My mistake, don't trip!"

"I'm not tripping, but I don't want you making fun of me," London whined.

"Dig this here," he cut her off. "Where is Kenya at anyway? Is she up there with Storm?"

London stopped pouting and refocused back on her plan. "Naw, she's not home. She went somewhere with Paris. Don't you and your girl communicate?"

"Don't worry about my girl, okay? That ain't none of your business." O.T. got closer, kissing her on the lips.

"Well, what is my business?" she replied with a sarcastic, sassy tone.

"This right here should be your main concern right about now!"

O.T. put her hand on his dick and backed her into the living room. It was just like Christmas and his birthday all wrapped into one as his dick got harder and harder. He had his hands roaming her entire body. London's skirt was pushed up, exposing the fact that she didn't have any panties on. Her naked ass looked just as he had imagined; perfect, plump, and round. After feeling on, across, and in every part of her body, O.T. was ready to get to the real deal. When he pulled his dick out of his jeans, London was amazed. His shit was long and thick. The head was lighter than the rest of it and was dripping.

"Come get this, ma, he wants to meet you." He motioned to her with one hand while slowly stroking his manhood with the other.

"Do you have any protection?" London wisely asked.

"Naw, I'm good. I ain't got no diseases!"

"I didn't say that you did, but I would feel a lot better if we used something." London spoke up as she broke free from his arms and ran upstairs to try to find a rubber in some of Kenya's belongings.

Five long minutes passed and London hadn't returned yet with the condom. An anxious O.T. sprinted up the staircase and bumped into London, who was coming out of Storm and Kenya's room. He held her tightly and began kissing her once again. She was breathing hard from searching the dresser drawers and was like a rag doll when he took his mouth off of hers. O.T.'s pants were still unzipped, making it easy for him to pull his semi-hard dick back out. He propped his body inside the doorway for support and pushed London down on her knees. Using both of his hands, he took her head in between them and guided her mouth onto the dome of his dripping stick.

"Give him a wet kiss," he urged.

"I haven't ever . . ." Her earring fell off from the force.

"Ever what?" He halted her words by rubbing his dick across her lips, making her taste his pre-cum.

The gloss that she had applied earlier was now on the head of his shaft. London tried to keep protesting, but was only met by O.T. placing his hand firmly behind her neck and the raw feeling of hard meat practically pounding her tonsils crooked. London was starting to make gagging sounds that only fired O.T. up more. The more that London fought to breathe, the harder he pushed in and out.

In all the erotic chaos that was taking place, the two of them failed to realize that for a few brief seconds, Storm had regained consciousness and reached out his hand toward them.

O.T. was at the point of no return and yelled out Paris's name, not London's, as he shot the mother lode down her throat, making sure that she swallowed every single drop. When he released her out of his strong-armed grip, London fell onto the plush, new-smelling carpet, gasping for air. Before she could regain her composure, O.T.'s phone chirped. It was Paris, saying that it was an emergency and to meet her at their house ASAP.

"I gotta go! Something's up and my baby needs me!" He stepped over London's body with his Tims still on to get a wet rag. O.T. then zipped up his pants on the way down the stairs, leaving a confused and emotionally drained and wounded London on the floor alone, whimpering.

"Please don't go," she quietly begged from the floor. "Please."

O.T. hadn't paid a second thought to anything that was being said. From the moment he got the call from Paris saying 911, nothing else mattered. "I'll be back to see Storm! And thanks for that head shot!"

London heard him slam the front door shut and the sound of the music from his car stereo fade out of ear range. After a short while she went to the bathroom.

London washed her face and brushed her teeth twice, trying to get the smell of O.T.'s thick, hot sperm out of her mouth. Every time she swallowed, it seemed like there was a strange aftertaste lingering. She couldn't believe that O.T. had the nerve to shout out another woman's name while they were doing something—well, at least while she was. London was totally pissed off, but not at him for that cold, callous display, but at Paris for interrupting them with her false problems.

London knew that Kenya would soon be on her way home, so she rushed to Storm's bedside to give him his medication and change out of her sister's clothes. She didn't want to hear Kenya's long, dragged-out arguing about anything tonight. She wasn't in the mood; besides, her throat was still hurting. The syringe was only one third of the way filled as London walked over to the IV bag that was hanging. She laid the needle down on the nightstand for a quick second to get one of the moist wipes out of the drawer and wet Storm's dry lips. Glancing over at the clock, she realized time was ticking and she still had to change back to her own clothes. As she reached over and started to touch Storm's face with the wipe, he suddenly raised his arm up, tightly grabbing her wrist.

"Kenya, how could you?" he managed to say through his dry lips.

"Stop—you're hurting me!" A stunned London tried pulling back. "Let me go! Let me go!"

"Why, Kenya—why did you lie to me?" Storm was now applying pressure to London's tiny wrist with every passing second.

"I'm not Kenya, I'm London!" she argued to no avail.

"Right, first you were Tasty, then Kenya, and now you're London!" Storm had tears swelling in his eyes. "I thought that you loved me? You said you did! You a liar!"

"I'm not Kenya I keep telling you! Now please let me loose." London tried prying his fingers off her. "You're hurting my arm, you monster!"

"You're not Kenya, but you're wearing the out-fit that I picked out for her in Vegas. You smell just like cucumber melon, her favorite scent, and if you haven't looked in the mirror lately, you look just like Kenya!" Storm was heated as he confronted who he truly believed was Kenya. "Stop denying it. Your lies won't work anymore. Just tell me why?"

"Please, Storm, you're hurting me!" London continued to plead, trying to break loose.

"You hurt me too!" Storm argued. "And I see the shit ain't stopped. I woke up and called out to you and what the fuck do I see, but my supposed-to-be fiancée and the love of my life on her knees deep-throating my baby brother." Storm snatched London by her neck. He was furious and wouldn't listen to a word that was coming out of her mouth. "I outta snap this motherfucker in two. You ain't shit!"

London found the inner strength somehow and yanked away from him, stumbling to the floor. "You're crazy!" she screamed, running out the room. "You're crazy!"

Storm tried his best to get out of the bed and chase after her, but he couldn't. His busted leg wouldn't let him. "Kenya! Kenya! Kenya!" he kept calling out in vain. "Come back here! Kenya, come back!"

The echoing sound of his voice and the thought of what he had witnessed between her and O.T. was too much for London to bear. She ran out onto the front porch to escape his verbal wrath. Ten minutes later Paris pulled up, letting Kenya out of the car and drove off in a rush. Kenya casually strolled up the walkway and found London perched on the stairs.

"What are you doing sitting out here?" Kenya's facial expression changed when she got a good look at her twin sister. "And why the hell do you have on my fucking clothes? Storm bought me that damn outfit! Go take it the fuck off!"

As Kenya waited for her answer, London grew angry at the fact that everything always had to be about Kenya. She twisted her upper lip and grinned. "You always think that you and your girl Paris are so high and mighty, don't you?"

"What that got to do with why you wearing my damn stuff?" Kenya fumed at her twin, trying to change the subject. "Tell me that!"

"Whatever!" London ignored her sister, while trying to wrap her head around what had just happened between her and not one brother, but two siblings.

"Well, I'm waiting." Kenya tapped her foot as if she was a scolding parent or teacher. "Why do you have my shit on your back and my new shoes on your feet? Are you gonna answer me or what?"

London stood up, rubbing her sore wrist that was starting to bruise and let her twin have it full blast. "I'll tell you what, Kenya. I've got a bright idea for you. Why don't you get your uppity, stuck-up, trying-to-forget-where-you-came-from-ass inside the house and try answering some questions your damn self?"

"What are you talking about?" Kenya was puzzled by her sister's statement. "What do you mean? Stop talking in secret, cryptic code all the time and try being normal for once."

"What I mean is that you should stop worrying so much about your damn precious little clothes that I borrowed and go in there." London pointed over her shoulder back toward the door. "Your foolish-ass boyfriend, Storm, is wide awake and seems to be somewhat in his right mind. And if I'm not mistaken, something tells me he wants to see you. Now, how's that for being normal!"

"Oh, my God! Move outta my way!" Kenya ran past London and up to her and Storm's bedroom. She could hear him screaming out her name louder with each step she took. It was now time for Kenya to face him, explain her ridiculous, unnecessary lies, and try her best to make shit right again.

15

You Dirty Bitch

Kenya neared the door of the bedroom, almost coming to a complete stop. She leaned against the wall, taking several deep breaths. Her pulse was racing and a sudden feeling of jitters caused her to tear up. Trying to get herself together, Kenya's ears were filled with the echoing of Storm's enraged yells.

"Kenya! Kenya!" he ranted and raved. "Where the fuck are you at? Don't let me get out of this motherfucking bed! I'm not playing around with your no-good ass!"

She was frozen with denial. Kenya had never once, since meeting Storm, heard him even raise his voice at her. Now he was lying a few feet away, injured and laid up in the bed, sounding like he was ready to break his foot off into her ass.

Damn! I can't put this shit off any longer. It ain't gonna do nothing but make matters worse. After one more deep breath Kenya turned the corner going in.

"Oh, I see your stankin'-ass finally decided to come back, huh?" Storm's hands were clenched onto the thin blanket that was on the bed. "I know you heard me calling you!" Kenya was quiet, not believing the bitter and callous words that were flying out of Storm's mouth. She couldn't move out the doorway as he continued to go off. "If my leg wasn't fucked up it would be me and you, ho, and mostly me! Believe that!" Storm struggled to get up without success, finally resting his weak body back on the mattress. "Bring your no-good, dick-sucking ass over here!" he demanded, firmly fighting through the excruciating pain he was in. Kenya remained still as tears of pain flowed down her cheeks. Silent, she had no response to him and his insults. She felt guilty enough for what he was going through. In reality, Kenya had no true, solid defense, because if she'd only been honest from the jump maybe some—if not all—the crap that her man had to suffer and endure could've been avoided totally. "I said come here, bitch! I swear to God I ain't gonna ask you no more, Kenya—bring your ass!"

"Wait, listen, Storm," she finally got the courage to say. "Please, baby, I can explain everything if you just give me a chance to."

"We been together for months on top of months. You had all the time in the world to confess your double, rotten-ass life and now you wanna be calm and talk."

"But—" Kenya tried once more to speak.

"But what, bitch? What the fuck can you say?"

"Please, Storm!"

"Please Storm, what?" he lividly hissed as he pounded his closed fist into the mattress. "Please don't be mad that I'm a backstabbing little whore? Is that what you wanna say after all this time—is it?"

Once again Kenya grew speechless. Terrified by his behavior, she still hadn't got within reach of Storm's bedside in fear of what he might actually do. Staring down at the carpet as she cried, she saw one of her earrings on the floor. Noticing it was the mate to the one that London was wearing; Kenya made a mental note to check her sister later on, knowing damn well that this wasn't the time.

"I guess you playing the dum-dum role now. Well, I'll tell you what, Kenya, consider all the fake games as over." Storm swallowed slowly, trying to regain his self-control. "You ain't gotta say shit, after all, the writing is already on the wall. Just know that because of you and your scheming I damn near got killed. Look what they did to me because of your wannabe-police ass!"

"Wait, Storm, are you going to give me at least a chance to try to make you see my side in all of this?" Kenya held up her hand, trying to reason with him. "Please, Storm. I'm begging you. Just listen."

"What you gonna tell me, huh?" He managed to laugh as Kenya gathered up the nerve to get a little closer to the man who she loved with all of her heart. "You gonna tell me that you ain't know nothing about that P.A.I.D. bullshit, right? You gonna tell me that you ain't trying to undermine my entire operation and shut shit down, right? Is that what you about to say Kenya—is it?"

Storm found some inner strength and reached out, yanking Kenya onto the bed with him. She didn't try to resist, feeling like if he kicked her ass and got it out of his system, maybe then he'd give her a chance to explain. Kenya was willing to make any sacrifice that it took to get things back to normal, even if it meant getting beat the fuck down in her own bed without putting up a fight. Storm tossed her around the king-sized bed with rage and fury as he kept the questions and harsh accusations coming.

"What's wrong, Kenya? I don't hear you telling me any more of those lies about you loving me so much!" he shouted as spit flew in her face. Yet Kenya didn't once scream or try to get away from the assault. "I guess you played me from the jump, huh?" Storm ripped Kenya's shirt off of her back, exposing her red-laced bra. The sight of her plump breasts usually excited him, but this time was much different. After seeing O.T.'s hands rubbing and feeling on them earlier as she sucked his dick, Storm wanted to throw up. Pissed at the sheer thought, he then smacked Kenya across her jaw with all his force. Not able to withstand the blow, she flew out the bed and hit the floor, dazed and dizzy. "Yeah, I guess you ain't London Roberts, either, with your good snitching rat ass?" Storm was enraged and out of control, as he threw the lamp off the nightstand at Kenya's head, "And I guess you wasn't just down on the floor swallowing my little brothers' dick damn near whole in front of my face neither, huh?"

Out of nowhere, the bedroom door flung open, causing both Kenya and Storm to turn and wait for the shit to hit the fan. The next round was sure to be worse than the first.

"Is that you, O.T.?" Storm asked as he wiped the sweat off his forehead. "Is it?"

Kenya planned on breaking the news about her twin sister, but the hell with it. She was now here to do it herself.

"No, it's not your henpecked little brother! It's me, London Roberts. The same London Roberts who was sucking his dick! Is that okay with you?" London stood with her hands on her hips, angrier than Kenya had ever seen her before in her life. "And if you touch my sister like that again I'm going to kill you with my bare hands!"

Storm's eyes seemed to be jumping out of their sockets. He rubbed them both, thinking that he must be hallucinating from the strong dosage of medication that they were keeping him doped up on. "I don't understand. What the fuck is going on?" He placed his palm on his forehead to check for a fever. "Kenya, who is she? I mean, which one of you is Kenya? I'm confused. What's going on? What are y'all trying to do to me? What is this?"

Storm started to hyperventilate from the shock and stress. He now was physically exhausted from struggling with Kenya. His body was still weak from his injuries and couldn't take the turmoil that was taking place. Without warning, he passed out cold.

It was a couple of hours later when Storm finally regained consciousness. O.T. was now sitting on the edge of the bed and laughing as his brother thankfully woke up once again.

"Open up your eyes, faggot-ass sleeping beauty. I ain't got all day to be waiting around to kick your pretty candy-sweet ass in the new Madden!" He teased as he normally did.

Storm was still slightly weak, but managed to sit up and get off into O.T.'s ass. "Later for all that. Man, where the fuck is Kenya at? I had one of the craziest dreams in the world, or should I say fucking nightmares. It was two of them bitches!"

"Hold up, dude, that wasn't no dream. It is." O.T. got his brother a cold glass of water to drink while he explained. "Your woman got an identical twin sister. Her name is London and trust me, you can't hardly tell them the fuck apart! Apparently, the girl been living back in Detroit all this time." O.T. shrugged his shoulders and rubbed his head. "Why didn't she tell you about her? I mean, that's wild. Kenya is straight out of order!"

"Fuck all that bull! Where is she at?" Storm asked loudly. "I don't believe all that twin stuff! Where the hell is she?"

"Who, London?"

"Hell naw, Kenya!" Storm frowned. "Matter of fact, yeah, go get both of them." He still didn't think that it could be possible that Kenya had a sister, let alone a twin sister. "Show me both of them side by side, then I'll believe that bullshit! Until then—"

"Yeah, all right then." O.T. left out the room and walked downstairs to inform the girls that Storm was awake. "Hey Kenya, he's up, but ol' boy don't think that it's two of y'all. He thinks that he was just bugging out on all that medication that Big Doc B got him hyped up on. He wanna see you and London, together."

"Well, too fucking bad! I don't want to see that no-good female-beating brother of yours!" London rolled her eyes as she kept a cold, wet rag pressed onto Kenya's swollen face. "After what he did to my sister I should call the damn police and press charges on him!" She leaped to her feet with anger.

"Bitch! I wish you would call five-oh on Storm!"

O.T. was now standing toe-to-toe with London, who wasn't in the mood for backing down. She still had a beef with him from earlier, but discussing that part would have to wait. Also sitting in the living room with a permanent grim expression was Paris. O.T. and his girl had been feuding ever since she stepped foot back inside their apartment. O.T., cold busted, had the nerve to try to lie about being at the mall with Chocolate Bunny. Even after Paris described stitch by stitch everything that the slut was wearing, just like a cheater, he still denied it.

Paris knew that her girl Jordan saw his ass, no doubt about it, but she wasn't gonna put her on front street or throw her up underneath the bus. Paris had just enough time to smack the shit out of O.T. and brace up to battle with his lunatic butt, when the call came in that Storm was awake and asking for him. The two promised to settle things up later that night as they put their differences aside and rushed over. Paris, fed up with his bully routine, got up in O.T.'s face, daring him to put his hands on London, Kenya, or her. O.T., feeling outnumbered, decided to try to reason with the hostile females, mainly Kenya.

"Listen, I don't know if all three of y'all is bleeding at the same time or what, but you gotta expect for Storm to be tripping right about now!" O.T. leaned over and looked Kenya in her eyes. "Don't none of us know what the fuck he had to go through and endure over there, do we? What the hell, that guy been shot, leg fucked the hell up, ear sliced, and almost starved to death, and you hoes wanna bug out because one of y'all got roughed up a little for starting all the bullshit from jump!"

Kenya was starting to feel remorse and guilt for having an attitude that Storm had kicked her ass without giving her a chance to talk. "I guess you're right, O.T." She removed the rag from her black-and-blue bruised jaw and got up off the couch. "Please, London, can you just go up there with me to see him for a minute?"

London folded her arms and turned her focus on the green grass and flowers that were right outside the huge picture window. She ignored her sister's request, acting as if the devil himself had asked for help burning Bibles on Easter Sunday morning.

"Get your punk-ass up them damn stairs before I drag you up there!" O.T. pushed London, who swung on him, but missed.

"Paris, I strongly suggest you get your coward so-called man before I say something that everyone will regret." London caught herself from falling into the sofa table. "Now that I think about it . . ."

Kenya remembered all the accusations that Storm made, including going down on O.T. and the fact that London owned up to it and even seemed proud. Kenya knew her twin's personality had turned foul and spiteful. She was in pain and sore, but knew that if London let that little cat out the bag, everybody in the house would be thumping.

"Please, London, I'm begging you." Kenya gave her the look, knowing exactly what her twin was only seconds from saying. "I'll do anything you want me to do. Just come on!" Kenya pulled her stubborn sister by the arm and led her up the staircase.

London turned back, giving O.T. the evil eye as she watched Paris start to argue with him.

The twins were almost at the bedroom door, when Kenya stopped and whispered in London's ear. "I know you and O.T. was fucking around this afternoon and that shit was rotten as hell. Me and you can kick it about that later tonight, but you got to promise me that no matter what, you won't go off on Storm. He was confused and he's still in so much pain, physically and mentally." Kenya held both of London's hands. "Please, London, be calm, for me!"

"All right—for you, Kenya I will and only you. I'll be on my best behavior, because as far as Storm and O.T. are concerned. I'm past being done!"

The twins joined hands as they slowly walked into the bedroom, making eye contact with Storm.

PARIS

"Damn O.T., why you always gotta go for bad all the time? Especially when it comes to females! Shit already fucked up enough without you trying to fight Kenya's sister because she don't wanna jump when you want her to." Paris was sick and tired of him and his wild ways. "I bet you don't be all mean-mugging and posted up in that nasty tramp Chocolate Bunny's face with that madness, do you?"

O.T. leaned back on the love seat and sucked his teeth like a woman. "I already told your ass I don't know what the fuck you talking about, so do me and yourself a favor and stop jumping to conclusions, blaming me for shit I ain't do before I really do backtrack and bang her black ass again!"

"You know what, you can do what the hell you want to do, but remember, two can play that game. It's nothing!" Paris took her purse off of the coffee table and nonchalantly made her way to the front door. "So think about that the next time your smart-ass goes missing in action!"

Paris started up her car and sped away, leaving O.T. looking dumbfounded.

"Kick rocks bitch!" he mumbled, walking upstairs.

16

It's True

"Hi Storm," Kenya spoke in a low, soft tone. "O.T. told me that you wanted to see me—or should I say *us*." She pointed over to London.

Storm, still extremely sore from earlier, sat all the way up in the bed, wiping his eyes. "Come here, Kenya. Come closer so I can see." The twins held each other's arms, carefully approaching Storm, who was shaking his head in disbelief. He squinted as the girls came closer to the light. "Shit! What kinda game is this?"

"Storm, I'm so sorry that I didn't tell you about London," Kenya begged, getting on her knees at the edge on the bed. "I just didn't think that you'd understand."

"What? Why not? Have I ever given you a reason to fear me, Kenya? Have I ever tried to control you? All this mess could have been avoided!" He came to terms the best he could.

"No." Full of shame she dropped her head to avoid eye contact with him, letting her hair drape over her distraught, battered face. "Never once, Storm."

"Then why?" he asked, keeping his eyes glued to London as he questioned Kenya. "What was the big fucking deal? Can you tell me that?"

The sound of him raising his voice caused London to speak up and intervene on her sister's behalf. "It seems as if to me that you have some kind of anger management issues. That trait must run in your family," London sarcastically added. "My sister probably didn't tell you about me because she figured that you would disapprove of anyone who wasn't agreeable with your criminal behavior or lifestyle."

"Oh yeah, is that right?" he fired back, not moved by her speech.

"It appears that way to me, especially by the looks of Kenya's face, you freaking animal!"

Storm had momentary forgotten about the harsh-ass kicking that he'd put on his girl. Remorsefully, he reached over, touching Kenya on her chin. "Look up at me." She obliged, hesitantly moving the hair out of her face, exposing the damage that would more than likely take days—maybe weeks—to heal. "Damn, Kenya! I'm sorry! I didn't mean to do all of that. You just caught me off guard." He then pulled her off the floor and onto the bed with him. "I'm sorry, baby girl."

"I know." Kenya nodded, accepting his apology. "I understand."

"Kenya! Please don't fall for that *I'm sorry* routine! If he hit you like that once he'll do it again! It might not be tomorrow or the next day, but it will definitely come again." London tried her best to discourage her twin from forgiving Storm.

"Why don't you try shutting the fuck up? It's your fault all this shit went down!" Storm barked, wishing he could strangle his woman's sister.

"My fault—are you sick in the head? I'm not the one out here running the streets, poisoning the damn community with drugs!" London yelled loud enough to wake the dead. "That would be you and your no-good brother who's guilty of that crime! You brought that wrath down on yourself!"

Storm tilted his head toward the side and had a flashback. "Oh, you mean the same brother who I saw you getting your knees dirty for earlier? Is that who you talking about?"

London was slightly ashamed, but continued her insults coming. "Yeah, that's him. He's also the same one that can get out of the bed and take a piss on his own! Not like you!" she teased with malice. "Damn bed wetter!"

"Oh, my God, London, no!" Kenya tried intervening, not believing the low blow her twin had just dished out.

"Kenya, I want this troublemaking whore out my motherfucking house!" Storm tried to get up out of the bed, but couldn't.

"Why don't you get your crippled morphine-ass up and put me out?" London challenged, knowing full well he couldn't.

"Bitch, get the fuck out! I'm not playing around with your stankin' wannabe-the-police-ass leave!"

Kenya stood up and broke up the below-the-belt insults that were taking place between London and Storm. "Listen, London, why don't you go back downstairs and let me speak to Storm privately? And Storm, why don't you try to calm down before you fall out again?"

"Okay, Kenya. I'll be in the living room." London looked back over her shoulder at Storm with disgust. "Don't let this animal taint your mind!"

"Try being out on the curb, whore!" Storm screamed out as London made her exit.

Almost at the end of the hallway she met O.T., who was busy talking to himself. "Excuse me!" She bumped his arm.

"Why the hell is you bugging? I thought me and you was tight! What's the problem?"

London couldn't believe that O.T. was so dense in the brain that he was truly convinced that his cold, heartless actions from earlier in the afternoon were acceptable. She went straight ghetto ham on him. "Okay, Negro! I'll tell you what the problem is!" She pointed her index finger in his face as her voice got louder. "If you think that you're gonna just mess around and toy with my feelings and emotions, you've got another thing coming, buster! And don't ever push me again!"

"Whoa! Slow the fuck down!" He brushed her hand away from his face. "I had to go. You heard Paris chirp me!"

"And?" London waited, head tilted to the side.

"And what? My girl needed me and I jetted. What else did you expect me to do?"

"Maybe show some type of love or affection toward me!"

"Come on now, London. Don't act like me and you is in some type of real relationship." O.T. stepped back, throwing his hands in the air. "You knew that Paris was wifey from the rip! She's number one in my world no matter how much I mess around!"

London was hurt once again as reality spit in her face. "Whatever! Ain't nobody thinking about you like that anyway!" She marched passed O.T. and stomped down the stairs.

"All these bitches bugging out today!" he laughed out loud as he went to check on Storm and Kenya.

When O.T. peeped in the room he saw that she was next to Storm, holding his hand. They seemed to be in deep discussion, so he didn't disturb them. O.T. went into the den and laid back on the couch as he looked over in the corner where the aquarium once sat that served as a final resting spot for Deacon's head. *Damn, I'm gonna hate to tell Storm about Deacon!*

It was now dark outside. It had started to thunder and pour buckets of rain, making the night seem to drag by. Storm and Kenya had been talking for hours, trying to get their lives back on track. Everything that she was holding in about her former life, he was now aware of. From the first morning she skipped school, Ty turning her out on the dance game, and even the fact that she pocketed the money that he and Deacon paid to Zack after her uncle and his crew shot up Heads Up. Kenya's life was now an open book.

Storm had no other choice but to confess about shit that he was holding back on also. Kenya sat silent as he talked about his mother's crack addiction, which he never did before. She was stunned to learn that Storm had once did time in a juvenile facility for killing his stepfather and worse than anything else, he revealed that he, O.T., and Deacon had all slept with Chocolate Bunny at one time or another back in the day. Kenya knew that O.T. had fucked the bitch, but not Deacon, and certainly not Storm.

Her hands were tied when it came to getting mad or passing judgments on his past, especially considering all her lies and the chain of events they set into motion.

What could she say, after all the terrible secrets and scandal she was tangled up into? Kenya had to remain calm and be understanding, even though she couldn't wait until she bumped heads with Chocolate Bunny again. All the "try to chill" information that she always begged Paris to do was out the window. By the time they were finished, Storm agreed to let London stay temporarily until all the bullshit was done and over. Kenya knew that it was gonna be a lot of fussing and confusion, but she loved both of them and wanted them both in her life.

Storm wanted to talk to O.T. about Deacon because Kenya kept avoiding any and all questions that involved his partner's name. Kenya went in the hallway and called out for O.T., hoping he was still there. When he finally showed up, she informed him that Storm wanted to see him and was asking about whether or not there had been any information concerning Deacon. O.T. entered the room and delivered the fucked-up, devastating news of Deacon's callous torture and murder.

When it was all said and done, Storm was speechless.

17

Mad Crazy

The months flew by and things only grew wilder and crazier by the moment. Storm was still in constant pain and hadn't stepped foot outside of the condo. He would have Kenya bring him home Tylenol 4's and Vicodin on the regular and kept a bottle of Rémy up to his lips, not being able to deal with his best friend's untimely murder. Even though Kenya would often beg and plead with Storm not to drink so much, especially while he was popping those pills, it was no use. He was obviously addicted and had started blacking out daily. His leg was still weak, so that meant that he was dependent on the aid of crutches, which messed with his mindset.

The fact that Storm was having trouble getting his manhood hard was also a major factor in his recovery. Most times he'd have to damn near beat his meat to death or choke and twist it to just make the motherfucker squirt piss. So him and Kenya getting it in like they used to was out of the picture altogether, driving him to drink harder.

Of course, London used that information to her advantage to taunt and tease Storm when he and she argued. What kinda comeback or response could any man have to that type of dis? Kenya, determined to make it work, would clean up behind Storm all day and manage Alley Cats at night. She was exhausted and drained each and every time her head would touch the pillow. She was nurse, maid, cook, and lastly referee between the still constantly-battling London and Storm. Her once-clear skin was now filled with pimples and dark bags were forming under both eyes.

O.T. and Paris were also still beefing. The shit seemed to never stop with them. O.T. was out running the streets harder than before. With Storm putting his own self on house arrest, that left O.T. to try to keep thangs pumping. That meant that every drop-off, every meeting, and every risk that went along with slinging dope was on his shoulders and his shoulders alone.

In between trying to be the self-proclaimed mayor of the hood, he still would squeeze in time to swing by and check on Storm. Those visits often would cause mad chaos to jump off at the condo when O.T. would see London. Kenya, knowing what she knew, was still on a strong mission to keep O.T. and London apart. She talked to a depressed and tearful Paris every night as she drove to the club. After the confrontation that she'd had at the hair salon with Chocolate Bunny, Kenya felt it best for the good of the club to let Paris go and get her head together. After all, it was only a temporary gig, so there were no hard feelings between the friends.

With O.T. gone so much, Paris would sit on the couch for hours at a time, watching old reruns of *Good Times* and stuffing herself full of candy, cookies, and chips, waiting for him to come back home.

London was having the time of her life as she sharpened her vocabulary skills Monday through Sunday, dusk to dawn, on an educationally disadvantaged Storm. They would find a reason to argue about rather the sun was shining at midnight or how many licks it really took to get to the center of a Tootsie Pop. All it took for the argument to be on was for the two to lay eyes on one another. For London, getting and remaining on Storm's bad side was second nature. She seemed to despise him no matter what he did or said. She even hated him when he was asleep.

Kenya felt that it was time for her sister to go back to Detroit or rather back to school, since the sale of the house was now final, but would never suggest it. Besides, they were keeping Storm's return kinda secret from the hustlers in the streets and with her and O.T. out and about, trying to hold things down, there was no one else that they trusted enough to keep somewhat of a watchful eye over Storm, especially with his blacking out from all the drinking.

FATE

It started off just like any other Friday night. Kenya was busy standing in the mirror, brushing her hair and getting prepared to head out to Alley Cats. She had on a pair of tight-fitting blue jeans and a blue and pink low-cut T-shirt with the words *Hot Shit* across the chest. Even with makeup on you could still see that she was worn out. Storm was lying, half asleep, in the bed with the television remote in his hand. An empty bottle of Rémy Martin was on the floor next to two 40-ounces of Olde English that were also bone dry. He was up to his usual behavior, getting drunk and passing out cold. Depressed and constantly belligerent, the once obsessed and overly attentive to his appearance man, hadn't shaved in days and as far as him taking a shower, that was almost an impossible feat.

The bedroom and the entire house, for that matter, smelled like a Texas roadhouse after a wild party. Kenya, never religious since Gran's death, prayed to God nightly that with time Storm would snap out of the destructive path that he was on and hopefully get his life back together and on the right track.

"Okay, sweetheart, I'm about to go down to the club." With the scent of cucumber melon lotion massaged deep in her skin, she lovingly nudged him on his arm. "Do you need me to get you something before I leave?"

Slurring, he reached out to grab her, almost falling out of the bed "Yeah, just you, Kenya! I want some pussy before you go!"

Kenya helped him all the way back up in the bed and played his request off, knowing that it had been months since he'd been home and his dick still couldn't get hard. Moreover, she had to go out and make the money and keep things going until her man got back on his feet and in his right mind. Kenya had no intentions on being late to Alley Cats because of one of Storm's pity parties that he was about to throw. "Look, I'll be back later. Why don't you go soak in the tub and chill out? I'll bring you a sandwich home from the club tonight—cool?"

"Naw bitch, why don't you bring me up another bottle of liquor and shut up your damn nagging?" He barked out orders like she was his slave and called her *bitch* so much she was beginning to think that was her name.

"Not a problem! I can do that." Kenya made her way into the den, yelling back to Storm. "I got you."

"Hey, London!" Kenya forced a smile as she saw her twin sitting at the desk, typing on the computer. "I'm about to leave and go to work. I know that this is asking a lot, but can you run to the store and get him something to drink?" Kenya pointed back toward her bedroom. "I'm late enough already."

"Don't you think that he's already had enough to drink for you, me, and the whole world?" London threw her hand up in her sister's face. "Your Prince Charming has turned into the village idiot, that much is obvious! He needs to get some help and you and his brother need to stop hand-delivering his poison."

"Sis, I know you're right, but I just don't know what to do. You know he ain't gonna humble himself and get help—well, not now anyways. So please, London, just this one time, for me?" Kenya begged, looking at her watch.

"Yeah, okay, let me get off Facebook with Fatima and I'll go."

Kenya, feeling like she had the weight of the world on her shoulders, walked passed the open bedroom door without as much as turning her head to say good-bye to Storm. *He's starting to get on my last nerve!*

***

London went into the kitchen to put away a few of the items that she bought from the corner store when she picked up a bottle for Storm. As she was bending down in the refrigerator to put the sodas on the door shelf, she felt a pair of hands snatch her body backwards, roughly knocking her down to the marble floor. *What the—! What's happening?* Her head struck the corner of the oak cabinet, making her woozy and somewhat confused. *Argg! Oh, my God!* When she regained her senses back she started to fight and struggle with a drunken, enraged, hallucinating Storm, who was now on top of her, licking her face. The more she wiggled, moving to get free, the greater pleasure he seemed to achieve.

"Don't fight with me, Kenya!" he drunkenly screamed in London's face with his nauseating, foul-smelling hot breath and scruffy beard rubbing against her cheek. "I told you Daddy wanted some, didn't I? Now give it to me!"

"I'm not Kenya, fool! I'm not Kenya! Get off of me! Get off!" she protested, trying to shove him off.

"I love you, girl! Why you acting like this after all I done did for you? Now give me some of that pussy you been holding out on!"

Storm ignored London's claims of not being Kenya and tried wrapping one of his huge hands across her mouth to silence having to hear anymore complaining or lies. London's eyes grew wide and bucked as her sister's fiancé held her down with the weight of his body. As he made use of his free hand to pull down his track pants so that his dick was dangling wildly between his and London's legs, she panicked. Her trying to knee him in the nuts was stopped by the force of him applying his total strength and body weight down on top of her.

"Are you crazy? Stop! Stop! Don't do this! Stop!" She fought until exhausted and out of breath from the struggle.

Storm was in some sort of a trance. It was like he was sleepwalking and totally unaware of his surroundings. His eyes rolled to the back of his head as he ripped London's shorts down and somehow shoved his hard dick up inside of her. It was the first, true 100 percent staying hard, can-bang-the-shit-out-of-you-all-night-long erection that he had since being back home and here he was on the kitchen floor, drunk as a son of a bitch with Kenya's sister's legs stretched wide open going in.

He acted like a madman as he went in and out of her overly moist pussy. All of London's outcries and claims of her not being her twin Kenya had come to a complete halt. She stopped resisting Storm and even seemed to start to enjoy what she was feeling. At one point she even closed her eyes and imagined that Storm was his brother O.T., making love to her. After two or three minutes of him having his way and doing his thang, Storm let out a yell as his body jerked and collapsed onto London's. After that, he passed out cold, not moving an inch.

Reality quickly set back in for her when the rotten-smelling musk of Storm's skin filled her nostrils. The ecstasy that she was just momentarily feeling had ended and now London wanted her sworn enemy the hell off of her. Somehow she managed to push his heavy body off onto the cold floor and got back up on her feet. The sight of Storm sprawled out, smelling like who done it and why, caused London to rush over to the sink and throw up all over the dirty dishes.

Damn! That felt good, but why did it have to be him? Stuff wasn't supposed to work out like this, London mumbled to herself as she stepped over his crutches that were blocking the door and walked out the kitchen to take a hot shower, leaving a snoring Storm to sleep his punk-ass on the floor. *But I sure see now why Kenya is putting up with all the crap that Storm is taking her through. I can't imagine what it feels like when he's sober.*

18

A New Day

The days that followed that night somehow brought about a drastic change in Storm's personality. He'd been woken up at four in the morning by Kenya returning home from work. He felt like warm, melted shit on a stick. Storm had no idea how he'd gotten downstairs, let alone on the floor. As he passed the huge oval-shaped mirror in the hallway, Storm caught a quick glance of himself and froze with disappointment at the sight. He saw a complete stranger staring back at him. It was then and there that he promised Kenya that he was gonna get his shit back right and 100 percent correct.

When he hugged Kenya his dick rose up, standing at attention, causing her to smile with excitement and anticipation of the possibility of what she'd been missing. The two of them made their way up the stairs and into their bedroom.

Kenya turned the shower on hot as she helped
Storm step inside. Having a new attitude, he
spent what seemed like hours scrubbing
months of built-up filth off his body. The com-
bination of the soap and the hot water caused a
mysterious deep scratch on the side of his neck
to sting.

Strangely, when he closed his eyes, Storm
kept seeing flashbacks of having sex with
Kenya on the kitchen floor in front of the open
refrigerator door. He knew that it must've been
a dream, so he dismissed it out of his mind.
No sooner than he was finished drying off, he
pounced on top of Kenya, making love to her
for the first time in months. She was in seventh
heaven as he freaked her from head to toe.
Kenya, unlike Storm who just had some pussy
earlier, hadn't had sex in what seemed like
twelve months of Sundays and was really feeling that shit. They went in 'til almost daybreak
while London, having had a brief taste of Storm
earlier, enviously listened to their loud moans
from the other room.

For weeks and weeks Storm stuck to his word
and stopped drinking altogether. The only fluid
that was now constantly up to his lips were
ice-cold water and the juices that flowed out of

Kenya's forever wet twat. O.T. had helped him hook the basement up with weights and other gym equipment that he needed to get back right to his usual self. Dedicated, he spent every free moment and waking minute on getting his body tight. As the days past, he was slowly gaining back the pounds and muscle mass that he'd lost while being held captive, then bedridden. He was transforming into looking like the old Storm who Kenya first fell in love with.

Even, to Kenya's surprise, London stopped complaining so much and being judgmental. She was being much more tolerant and civil to Storm as well. The two of them weren't arguing as much and London was even sharing responsibilities, helping Kenya out with the housework more often. Yet poor, naive Kenya had no idea that the true reason London was lending a helpful hand was so that she could smell Storm's T-shirts and dirty underwear every chance she got. The high point of London's day would come when she'd carry the laundry basket in the basement to wash and get an up-close and personal show of Storm's perfect body pumping iron.

"Girl, thanks for looking out for me with some of this cleaning." Kenya hugged her twin, happy that things were settling down. "You know Gran blessed you with all the secrets in keeping a neat house, anyhow."

"Oh, it's nothing," London winked at her twin, being sarcastic. "What's yours is mine, so I wouldn't leave you hanging. Like I said, it's nothing."

"Yes, it is. I want you to know that you're really appreciated and that I love you, London!"

"We sisters, girl!" London gave Kenya a half-hearted smile and a hug, smelling Storm's scent on her twin's shirt. "You should know by now that I've got your back."

The two finished getting the condo together because they were having a special dinner later that evening. It would be Kenya, Storm, Paris, O.T., and London. Kenya trusted in the changes that were taking place in London when it came to O.T. It seemed just like a snap of the finger, London was no longer attracted to O.T. It would be days when O.T. stopped by to hang out with Storm that London wouldn't even come out of her room to even say hello. She stayed asleep most days, acting as if she didn't have a care in the world. She'd stopped talking about returning to college or Detroit altogether.

Whatever jumped off to keep the two of them from messing around again behind Paris's back, Kenya was overjoyed and didn't question it. She never did get around to having a long conversation with London about what really went down the day that Storm saw her and O.T. in the hallway, so Kenya let her imagination work for itself, then put it completely out of her mind. Putting two and two together was easy. But nevertheless, things were back on track all around, with the small exception of the ongoing Paris, O.T., Chocolate Bunny saga, which was a hot topic that raged on nightly at the club.

The table was set and everything was picture-perfect for the evening. Kenya, with London's help, cooked enough food to feed a small-sized army. The huge celebration feast consisted of everything from hot country fried chicken, pot roast smothered in homemade brown gravy and catfish, to fresh collard greens, candied yams, and black-eyed peas. The girls had outdone themselves just as their grandmother had taught them.

Paris and O.T. arrived to the condo on time. They planned on having an early supper because Kenya was due down at the club by eight that evening and couldn't be late. She tried to get someone to fill in for her, but had no success. She was the only voice of reason at the club and things had a habit of going crazy when she wasn't there. O.T. wasted no time disappearing into the basement where Storm was just finishing up his workout, leaving all three females alone in the kitchen area.

"Hey, Paris," London spoke as she inspected her sister's best friend's shape. Paris had packed on at least fifteen pounds or more since London had last seen her. "What have you been up to lately? Where have you been hiding?"

"Not much." Paris shrugged her shoulders. "I've just been taking it easy, trying to get my mind right."

"Oh, okay, it's just that I haven't saw you around here very much." London grilled her sister's best friend, still stunned by Paris's big physical change. "Is all well with you?"

Kenya saw the direction that her slick-mouthed twin was headed and jumped in to rescue Paris from all the questions. "Do me a favor, London." Kenya wiped her hands on the plaid-colored dish towel. "Can you go and call the fellas up while me and Paris start bringing the food to the table?"

"Yeah, I can do that." London happily left to go in the basement. If she was lucky, maybe Storm still had his shirt off. The aroma of the various foods was making her dizzy anyway, as well as the intense heat from the oven.

When London was clearly out of ear range, Kenya apologized for her twin sister being so damn nosy. "Girl, she didn't mean to be all up in your shit like that. She just was concerned, that's all. She don't know any better."

Paris grabbed one of the china platters with the chicken on it and headed toward the brightly-lit dining room. "Don't worry. I don't mind. I guess I do look like a mess with all this extra weight that I'm hauling."

"Stop tripping, you tight, girl." Kenya followed behind her friend with a big bowl of greens in her hands.

"You don't have to lie. I know that this fat shit ain't cute." Paris lowered her head in shame, on the verge of tears. "But I can't help it. That fool got me so messed up in the head I can't think straight half the time!"

"Stop being so down on yourself."

"I can't help it, Kenya! Do you know that O.T. hasn't touched me in over two and a half weeks now?" Kenya consoled her friend as she sobbed. "He barely even comes to the crib until daybreak. He claims that he's out hustlin', but I know that nigga is lying. He cheating with some ho!"

Before Kenya got a chance to hear the entire story, London returned with both guys trailing behind.

"Damn, that shit smells good!" Storm rubbed his flat-abs as he took a seat at the head of the long marble table. "I'm about to throw the hell down!"

O.T. followed his brother's lead and sat at the other end. After all the food was laid out and the girls sat down, Storm blessed the gathering before the first fork was placed to anyone's lips. Two or three seconds after that the shit was on! The guys acted like they'd never had soul food before as they devoured everything that they piled on their plates, getting seconds and even thirds of some dishes. The only dinner conversation that was taking place consisted of girl talk and the sounds of grunting.

It was close to seven and the group was just about done with eating. Kenya was bringing an apple pie to the table for dessert when O.T.'s cell phone started to ring, causing Paris to suddenly flip out.

"Damn! Can we have one day in peace when that ho of yours ain't blowing up your fucking phone?"

"Don't start with me, Paris. I ain't in the mood for that dumb shit now!" Fed up with her constant accusations, O.T. walked away from the table shaking his head. "I've got something to go handle."

"Yeah, right!" Paris reached back, trying to hit him as he walked passed. "You ain't shit but a cheating liar. We all know! The people at the club know! The people in the street know! Hell, even the old Chinese lady at the dry cleaner's knows you a cheating piece of garbage!"

Kenya leaned over and wrapped her arms around Storm's neck, who was still seated at the table. "Baby, oh, my God, can you say something, please?"

"I love you like a motherfucker, Kenya, but I don't get in the middle of no couple's bullshit." Storm cut himself a piece of pie as he remained silent, watching his baby brother and Paris go at it. "And trust me, you don't need to either!"

London was especially enjoying the long evening observing both couples at each other's throats. At first she felt like a third wheel and out of place; now she was happy not to be either of the girls.

O.T. took Paris's car keys off the couch and trotted out to her car, leaving her stranded without a ride to get home.

"Damn, I hate him! I swear I do!" she huffed.

"Don't worry, girl. I'll drop you off on my way to Alley Cats." Kenya patted her friend on the back as she snarled at Storm, who was still nonchalantly stuffing his face with pie. "Just let me grab my purse and we'll be out."

Paris and Kenya left London and Storm home alone. On the ride to drop her off at her and O.T.'s apartment, Kenya was having a hard time trying to comfort an almost panic-stricken Paris. The loud, piercing cries from her were coming close to causing Kenya to swerve off the highway. She already needed a few aspirin for the headache she was suffering after her disagreement with Storm, but this was much worse.

"Why don't you go inside and try to get some rest? It's been a long day." Kenya tried her best to convince Paris to calm the hell down, go inside, lie down, and relax.

"You right, girl. I'm just gonna go in there and chill 'til his ass comes home—then trust, it's back on!"

Kenya blew the horn once as she drove off toward Alley Cats.

LONDON

"Dang, I guess this dinner party is over, huh?" Storm was polishing off his last piece of pie that was on his plate, not paying attention to a word coming out of London's mouth. "Are you listening to me?" London threw a napkin at Storm to get his attention. "Can you speak or what?"

"Dang, slow your roll, London. Can a guy eat his dessert in peace or what?" Storm pushed his chair back from the table and patted his bloated, full stomach. "Y'all females around here doing way too much for me tonight. Well, I might as well go in the basement and do a little cardio to work this shit off."

"Excuse me. Despite what all of you people around here think, I'm not the damn maid!" London grew infuriated that she was ultimately left the task of cleaning up.

"Where the hell is you going with this bull-shit? I know your ass know for a fact that I ain't about to bust no suds for nobody." Storm stretched out his arms, yawning. "So, for real, if that's where you going with this conversation, you can cut that mess out right now!"

"Forget it! Just go work out with your lazy self!"

"Lazy? Wow, your ass is the one that needs to hit the gym. I mean, I ain't being in your business, but you is getting a little thick around the waist, London! You and that damn Paris both getting out of order and need to hit a gym."

"Just go somewhere, lazy Negro, while I clean up!"

"Come on now, London, is this the body of a lazy motherfucker?" He lifted his shirt, expos-ing his eight-pack abs.

London controlled herself from leaping across the table and attacking Storm the same way he'd attacked her months earlier. "Whatever!" She looked the other way as quickly as possible and started removing the dishes, taking them in the kitchen. Once again, she started to feel dizzy and stumbled.

Storm felt sorry for her and grabbed a few of the dirty plates and followed in the kitchen behind her. When he turned the corner he saw London bending over in the refrigerator putting stuff away and had a brief flashback. "Damn! Why do I keep seeing that shit?"

"Did you say something?" London stood up, turning around to face him.

"Naw, I was just talking to myself." Storm shook off his strange thoughts as he rubbed the deep scar that was still on his neck.

"Does it still hurt?" London smirked, starting the hot dishwater in the sink. Her heart was beating double-time as she experienced flashbacks of her own. After all, they were back to the scene of the crime, so to speak. "It was pretty deep."

"What are you talking about? What you know about my neck?" Storm was puzzled that she'd even noticed him touching it.

"You can cut all the games out, Storm. It's been months and you see I haven't said a word to anyone. It's our little secret."

"Huh?" Storm was confused and his facial expression showed. "Stop playing around and tell me what the fuck you trying to say?"

"Come on now, are you serious? You don't remember?" London glanced down at the floor and raised her eyebrows.

"Remember what?" he asked again. "What the hell is your crazy-ass talking about now?"

"I've got to finish washing dishes." London laughed, still not believing that Storm had truly forgotten their sexual encounter. "We'll talk about it later—one day."

Storm left out the kitchen and headed toward the basement to try to figure out what his woman's twin sister wanted him to remember. *Whatever the hell it is, something tells me it can't be nothing good!* After months of being sober, Storm snatched a bottle of Rémy off the bar cart to keep him company and help him possibly remember.

19

I'm In Shock

Shit, it's crowded already. Kenya pulled
around to the other side of the parking lot to
make sure that security was patrolling the
entire perimeter. She cut her lights off so she
wouldn't draw attention to herself as she crept
up. What she saw next made her headache
start to pound worse. It was O.T. sitting back in
Paris's car, talking to Chocolate Bunny, who was
leaning in the window practically in the driver's
seat.

After five minutes of her watching their every
movement like a hawk, Kenya wanted to beat
the shit out of Chocolate Bunny her damn self.
Matter of fact, she wanted to stump O.T. in his
fucking ball sack for playing with her girl Paris's
emotions. She knew it was time for her to step
in and do something about Chocolate Bunny
once and for all. "This idiot gonna mess around
and get AIDS one day," Kenya snarled under her
breath, as she looked at Chocolate Bunny stuff

some cash in her bra and wave to O.T. as he peeled out in Paris's car. "Flat out, I gotta get rid of that black no-good gutter rat."

"Hey Kenya, what's the game plan for tonight?" The head of security, Boz, was busy trying to get things straightened out before things really got off the hook.

"Same old same." She looked up toward the center stage at Jordan shaking her ass in front of a group of middle-aged customers who were posted on perverts' row. "Just make sure that all the girls circulate around the club and don't spend all night catering to one fool trying to slow pimp all his cash."

"You got it, boss. I'm on top of it!" he reassured Kenya. "Don't worry about nothing. I got you!"

Everything was flowing smoothly on the nightshift. Kenya sat on her favorite seat at the long bar and observed the crowd enjoying themselves. Most of the dancers were either up in VIP or humping on a guy's lap, doing something strange for some change. The DJ was working the high-priced light system and had the sounds spinning. It would definitely be a good moneymaking night for the club.

"If you fellas' nature stood tall and hard for that last honey that worked that brass pole, you'll love this next prime-time delight. Alley Cats is home base to this lovely dark meat. She's the warmest, wettest, freakiest thang walking around these-here parts." The DJ dimmed the lights low as he got the crowd going. "Chocolate Bunny, bring your wide twerkin' ass up on that center stage and do the damn thang!"

Kenya walked behind the bar and poured herself a small glass of wine. She studied Chocolate Bunny dancing and wondered what it was that made men like her. In Kenya's opinion she wasn't sexy or cute. The only thing that Kenya saw in the whore was that she had a big butt; a big butt that seemed to be spreading out a little bit more than normal for her taste, but the tramp was still bringing in revenue to the club and at the end of the day that was all that mattered. In her line of business, cash was king.

As Kenya sat drinking her second glass of wine, her opinion about the constant thorn in her and Paris's side started to change. *That tramp is gaining too much weight. Matter of fact, I'm gonna give her trick-ass a few weeks off to drop that shit or get fired altogether.* Kenya finally found a way, after months of plotting, to get Chocolate Bunny out of Alley Cats without Storm or O.T. feeling like it was being done out of spite. After all, rules were rules. Each dancer had to maintain a certain look to be on the schedule and it was plain to see Chocolate Bunny was no longer fitting that status. *As soon as she goes back to the dressing room to switch up on her outfits, I'm gonna break the bad news to her trifling butt.*

Kenya raised her glass to her perfectly glossed lips and slowly sipped the rest of her wine. After two more songs dancing on center stage, Chocolate Bunny was done with her set.

CHOCOLATE BUNNY

"I'm happy for you," Jordan lied with a straight face. "What are you going to name the baby? Is it a boy or a girl?"

"It's gonna be a boy. I'll probably name him after his big-head daddy." Chocolate Bunny was in the dressing room, bragging about being pregnant and the fact that her and her mystery man had just put a huge down payment on a new house.

She wasn't fooling everyone with all that top-secret hush-hush shit about the baby's daddy. All the girls in the club would see her all up in O.T.'s face day in and day out, laughing and giggling. They weren't blind or stupid. Jordan tried her best to pry the private information out of Chocolate Bunny or at least make her slip up and finally admit the shit, but wasn't successful. She was keeping that close to the vest.

"This week is gonna be my last grindin' up in this here motherfucker. My man wants me to sit on my ass and raise his son." Chocolate Bunny affectionately stared down at the tiny bulge that was growing and smiled. "I'm ready to retire out this game anyway and get my life back together. Maybe I'll go back to school or something productive like that."

Kenya was at the doorway ear hustling on the conversation that was taking place between Jordan and Chocolate Bunny. She felt like marching in the dressing room and knocking that bastard-ass baby the fuck out of the stomach of that man-stealing black-snake bitch, but what good would that really do? Paris would still be devastated whenever O.T. would be man enough to break the news to her. *He should've just broke up with her a long time ago and saved her the grief of all the drama.* Kenya eased away from the door, unnoticed, and sat back down at the bar. She had the bartender give her the entire bottle of wine and poured herself another glass. *This shit is fucked up,* was all that kept racing through her mind.

Kenya decided by her fourth glass that it'd be better to keep this baby-crap information from Paris as long as possible to spare her feelings. Considering the unstable, depressing state of mind and constant stress that Paris had been dealing with, Kenya was terrified what would be her best friend's response to all the madness that was going down. Luckily, this was gonna be Chocolate Bunny's last week dancing, so she claimed. But just in case she had any thoughts of prolonging her departure from Alley Cats, the sooner Kenya made it official and fired her low-down sneaky-ass the better. She'd call Chocolate Bunny right before her shift the next day and let her know what was really good.

"Last call for alcohol!" the DJ announced for the last and final time for the night.

It was damn near two in the morning and the strip club was slowly clearing out as the house lights came on. All the girls were going back to the dressing room to get changed and go home or wherever they planned on laying their head down for the night. Some had boyfriends waiting, some had husbands, some had tricks, and even a few had a bitch. Whatever the case was, everyone was hauling ass to leave out.

"All right, Addiction and Tight-n-Right, I'll see you ladies tomorrow." Boz held the door open and watched them to their vehicles.

"Hold up, Boz, I'm ready to jet too!" Chocolate Bunny yelled out while struggling with her duffel bag, followed by a loud-talking Jordan.

"Yeah, me too! I'll holler at y'all in a few!" Boz saw Jordan and her woman embrace, kiss, then drive off.

Chocolate Bunny seemed to be enraged as she threw her bag to the pavement. "What kinda jealous-hearted-ass ho done did some treacherous shit like this?" Chocolate Bunny fumed, looking down. "And Boz, where the fuck was security at?"

Boz walked over to investigate and found all four of Chocolate Bunny's tires slashed. "Damn, girl! Who the fuck did you piss off tonight?"

"You know how these bum bitches up here be hating on me because I clock major dollars up in this motherfucker!" Chocolate Bunny screamed across the parking lot to make sure that the rest of the dancers who hadn't left yet could hear exactly what she was saying.

"Fuck you!" one of them replied as they all laughed at her misfortune and went on about their way.

Chocolate Bunny whipped out her cell, rolled her eyes, and pushed number one on the speed dial. "Hey baby, it's me!"

"Where you at?"

"I'm still at the club!"

"Why you still there? I was waiting for you."

"One of these tramps done sliced my tires!"

"Well, just turn the sounds on and sit tight. I'm gonna send one of my street soldiers to find a nigga with a flatbed and come get you. I told you ya ass need to be done with that club!"

"Don't start with me, okay, sweetie? I love you!"

"I love you too! You and my son!"

"Okay, see you soon!"

Twenty minutes or so had passed and Chocolate Bunny was still sitting in her car, waiting. Boz was chilling on the hood, keeping her company as long as possible. Kenya finally appeared at the door and waved for him to come inside. It was time to pay the security detail for the night and close up, so he had to return to his post and finish up club business.

"You better come in the club and wait in there," Boz suggested as he opened the car door wide for Chocolate Bunny to get out. "I can't abandon your ass out here with all these perverts and stalkers roaming the streets!"

"Yeah, you ain't never lied. I don't want nobody to kidnap my fine black perfect ass!" she joked as they both walked back into Alley Cats.

Kenya was going over the paperwork and having each guy sign for his pay envelope. Boz had to do his job and verify each bouncer's nightly evaluation. As soon as Kenya was done with her part, she then focused on Chocolate

Bunny, who was sitting at the other end of the bar playing one of the poker arcade games.

"Hey, girl, what's the deal?" Kenya interrupted her game, feeling like now was just as good a time as any to fire her.

"Nothing, just waiting for my sweetie to send a tow truck to come rescue me from them broke tricks slicing my damn tires! You know I'm off tomorrow, so I'll call the club in a few days to talk to you about something! It's kinda important."

"Well, I'm sorry about your tires, but this gives me the opportunity to kick it with you about something else. It's important too."

"Oh, yeah? Well, what is it, Kenya?" Chocolate Bunny smartly asked. "What the hell did I do wrong now? I'm dying to know!"

"Nothing, we just need to talk. Give me a minute to finish things up and send the fellas home so we can have some privacy."

"Yeah girl—whatever!" Chocolate Bunny put another quarter into the game to pass away the time waiting for the tow truck to arrive. She was gonna just tell Kenya over the phone she quit, but fuck it—now was as good a time as any. Fuck waiting any longer.

Boz and the rest of the guys gathered their stuff and left out with a few beers in hand. "Are y'all gonna be all right?" he turned back, asking before he started his truck.

"Yeah, we good," Kenya waved him off. "Go ahead and bounce. Go home to your family. I'll see you tomorrow evening!" Kenya shut the front door, making sure that it was locked. Ready to argue, she then took a seat next to Chocolate Bunny and braced up for round one. "Listen chick, I swear to God that I'm not trying to be twisted all up in your business, but I think what you been doing is seriously foul and wrong as a motherfucker."

"Excuse me, but what in the hell am I supposed to be doing, Ms. Thang?"

"Don't play silly mind games with me, Nicole. I was coming in the dressing room and heard what you said on the humble."

"And please tell me, just what do you think you heard?" Chocolate Bunny snickered as she leaned back on the stool, getting an earful.

Kenya was getting angry at the brazen and heavy-mouthed Chocolate Bunny. "So you about to have a baby, huh?"

"And so what? What's it to you?"

Before Kenya could answer they heard a noise come from the rear of the club. Both of them froze, looking at one another with a sense of fear, because they knew for a fact that everyone had left the building. Kenya kicked off her high heels and quietly made her way around to the other side of the bar, grabbing the pistol that they kept on the bottom shelf. Two seconds later she and Chocolate Bunny heard the noise once again.

"Whoever the fuck is back there, you about to catch some serious hot ones in the ass!" Kenya screamed out into the rear of the club. "I'm not bullshitting! You best to come out! We already done called the police!"

Chocolate Bunny and Kenya's mouths both almost dropped to the ground in disbelief when the person emerged out of the dark shadows and into the light. It was a red-eyed, worn-out, and exhausted-looking Paris. She had her nightgown and slippers on while a huge 9 mm pistol graced her side. Her hair was all over her head and her puffy face was full of tears. "It's me, Kenya!" She dropped the spare club keys on the bar. "Don't worry, it's only me!"

"Girl, damn! Why the fuck is your ass lurking like that?" Kenya, relieved, lowered her gun. "I could've shot you. And damn, why you dressed like that? And shit, why you here?"

"Damn, she's right. Are you crazy or what? Have you lost your mind?" Chocolate Bunny jumped in, confused also.

Paris's fingers tightly gripped the gun handle with animosity. "You don't say shit to me, man-stealing ho!"

"Who the fuck is you talking to like that? I 'bout done had enough of you tripping out whenever the fuck you feel like it! Not to mention putting your damn hands on me like at the salon!"

Kenya knew that Paris was out of her mind and didn't know what exactly she had planned on doing, so she did her best to try to defuse the situation before it got well out of hand. "Listen, why don't we all just calm down?" She raised her hands up in between Paris and Chocolate Bunny.

"Oh, I'm good!" Chocolate Bunny replied, as she looked Paris up and down, shaking her head. "I'm not the fool that's standing in a strip club in the middle of the night rocking pajamas with my wig tore up."

"Paris, why are you here anyway?" Kenya wondered, asking her friend. "And girl, why aren't you dressed? What's wrong with you? What happened?"

"I didn't have time." Paris was timid in her demeanor and response when talking to her best friend.

Kenya, tired of trying to figure her girl's motives out, threw her hands up in the air. "I'm confused as hell! I give up! What's going on? What's wrong? Tell me!"

"This whore right here is what's wrong with me!" Paris pointed at Chocolate Bunny with her pistol. "She's what happened!"

"Look, you lunatic, it'll be in your best interest to stop waving that gun around before it mess around and go off, then it really will be some shit!" Chocolate Bunny put her hands on her hips, showing no signs of fear of Paris and what she could possibly do.

Kenya stood back, realizing that her best friend was on some other type of shit and had totally and officially snapped. "Just tell me what happened? I thought that you were at home sleeping—relaxing?"

"I was at home doing what you said until Jordan called me!" Paris wept like a small child not getting toys on Christmas morning.

It then hit Kenya like a ton of bricks what the fuck this whole scene was about. Jordan must've called Paris with that baby bullshit getting in her head and getting her fired up. "Listen, Paris, I was gonna tell you, but I just found out myself—tonight."

"Look, y'all, I hate to break up this wild soap opera y'all living in, but I'll be out in my car waiting for my man's people," Chocolate Bunny blurted out. "Ain't nobody got time for you or you!"

"Bitch, I swear on everything I love, if you take one step that's your black-cheating-ass!"

"Yeah, okay Paris, can you just tell a girl, with your messy self, what the fuck this is all about, if you don't mind? I'm listening!"

Paris wiped her tears, gathering up her courage to hear Chocolate Bunny finally confess the truth. "So I heard you supposed to be having a baby?"

"Yeah, and?" Chocolate Bunny put her hand on her stomach. "What about it? Is that okay with you? Matter of fact, why do you even care so damn much?"

"Why the fuck would you think that the shit would be okay with my ass?" Paris hissed with anger and contempt.

"Girl, bye! I ain't gotta clear my personal life with either one of you two messy bitches. Y'all be buggin'!" Chocolate Bunny shifted her weight on one hip. "So deal with it! I'm having a baby—so fucking what!"

"So you ain't denying it?" Paris shouted nervously as her hand shook and her words echoed throughout the empty club. "You're pregnant?"

Chocolate Bunny started moving her fingers, acting as if she knew sign language. "Yes . . . dumb . . . bitch! I . . . am . . . going . . . to . . . have . . . a . . . baby!" She dragged out each syllable of each word while laughing. "Now . . . fuck . . . you!"

"Naw, fuck you!!!" Paris raised the gun up and started to cry hysterically. "I can't take this bullshit no more! I'm sick and tired of y'all playing me for a fool. Now you about to have his seed and throwing it up in my face!"

Chocolate Bunny saw her chance and took it, bum-rushing Paris, causing them both to tumble to the floor. Kenya watched helplessly while the two rivals fought and wrestled for the gun. She couldn't tell who was getting down the best and had no intentions on trying to get a closer look and maybe risk getting shot by mistake. All Kenya could do was clench her own gun tight and wait for the outcome.

"Now what, you crazy psycho bitch? Where is all them empty threats at now? Huh? Where they at?" Chocolate Bunny had come out on the top and now had possession of the gun. "Talk all that la-la shit now so I can bust a cap in your silly-ass! I'm tired of all your over-the-top antics!" She was trying to catch her breath with each passing word she justifiably screamed.

Paris was also out of breath from the struggle and her sorrowful crying had gotten louder. Kenya, out of desperation of what could possibly take place next, had no choice but to put one up top and point her gun at a now frantic, roughed-up and bruised pregnant Chocolate Bunny.

"I'm confused! Why is y'all hoes so worried about my son and me being knocked up, period? Am I making that much money for this club that y'all bugging out like that cause y'all gonna lose dough?" She panted repeatedly as a sharp, piercing pain unexpectedly shot throughout her lower belly. Chocolate Bunny then grabbed her side with her free hand and

moaned out in agony. "His daddy is gonna—"
Before she could get the words out another pain
set in this time worse than the first.

"Son?" Paris whined, not believing what she'd
just heard her sworn enemy say. "You having a
boy—a son?"

"Oh no! Oh, my God!" Kenya pointed to the
floor. "Look!"

Chocolate Bunny had streams of dark blood
running down her leg. It had started to form a
huge puddle right beneath the spot where she
was standing. Her once-white skirt was not only
dirty from the filth that was on the club floor,
it was now soaked and stained with her own
blood. Reaching her free hand up in between her
legs, she felt her pussy. When Chocolate Bunny
pulled her trembling hand back, it was covered
in thick red and dark-burgundy mucus. Still
having pain in her stomach area, the distraught
mother-to-be smeared the foul-smelling clots
on her skirt and instantly went the fuck off.

"You killed my baby! You killed my baby!" Her
eyes grew wide with panic and death raged in
her heart. "You jealous dirty rotten crazy bitch!"

Chocolate Bunny pointed the gun directly at
Paris's head and was seconds away from pulling
the trigger as Kenya quickly let off two rounds,
knocking Chocolate Bunny off her feet, slamming her already battered body to the ground.
The first bullet struck the pregnant female dead
in the stomach, more than likely taking the

baby out of the game for sure, while the other bullet found its mark in her collarbone.

Chocolate Bunny squirmed for a few good seconds, then moaned out softly. As she took her last breath and slowly released all her bodily fluids onto the strip club's floor, Kenya and Paris stood in disbelief, not fully grasping what they had just both taken part in.

"Oh shit! I can't believe this!" Kenya lowered her gun, taking a long, deep breath. "That stupid girl made me do that dumb shit! She made me shoot her!"

Paris just stood in the same spot, not moving, mouth wide open. Kenya, still shaken, tossed her pistol onto the bar and went to get the other one that was still clutched in Chocolate Bunny's hand. Kenya then very carefully slid her finger off the trigger, placing it with the other gun.

"What are we gonna do now?" A dazed Paris finally spoke.

"We gonna get rid of this black bitch, that's what we gonna do now!"

"Okay, but how?" Paris was usually hardcore and a ridah, but lately she'd been punkin' out and scared of her own shadow.

"Listen, pay attention. Just go in the back storeroom and get me that big roll of plastic that the painters left and the jug of industrial bleach," Kenya ordered with authority. "And hurry up before this girl bleeds even more on my floor."

"Okay Kenya, I'm going!" Paris wasted no time as she ran toward the back of the club.

They rolled Chocolate Bunny onto the plastic and dragged her lifeless body over near the back door. Kenya had a scalding hot bucket of water and plenty of rags. Paris poured the strong bleach across the area and held her nose. It was supposed to be mixed with three parts water, but Kenya wanted it straight. Both girls' eyes burned as they scrubbed the spot Chocolate Bunny had taken her last breath in.

The club's floor was now spotless and there were no visible signs that a murder had just taken place. Kenya's car was already parked in the rear of the building in her reserved spot, so all they had to do was get Chocolate Bunny the hell out of there. It took ten long, hard minutes of tugging, yanking, and pulling to get her body stuffed and wedged behind the Dumpster that had just been emptied the night before. Paris took some of the plastic and balled it up, placing it in a bag. On the way home she intended on disposing of it in someone else's garbage can on the other far side of town.

Kenya went back inside the club, grabbing both guns off the bar along with Chocolate Bunny's purse and Paris's set of club keys. Snatching the security camera tapes, she then put them all in a small bag and doubled it. After double-checking the entire interior once again for any other evidence they might've overlooked, she set the alarm system and jumped into the car with Paris. As they drove off in the other direction, they could see the flashing lights of a flatbed tow truck that was pulling into the club's parking lot.

"Damn, that was too close!" Kenya kept glancing in the rearview mirror to make sure they weren't being followed.

The ride to Paris's house was silent after that. Neither of the girls said a word to the other. They were about one mile short of getting to their destination when a police car got behind the two cold-blooded murderers. Kenya knew not to tell Paris that the cops were behind them because she knew that she would undoubtedly spaz out and get them flicked for sure. Luckily at the next traffic light the cops turned off, going on their way. When the pair finally got in Paris's driveway, Kenya turned to her and stuck her hand out.

"What?" Paris squinted her eyes at Kenya.

"Give me any more sets of them motherfucking keys you got stashed somewhere to Alley Cats, before your ass decides to come back in that bitch another night and lay another dancer to rest for messing around with that no-good cheating O.T.!" Kenya shook her head.

"Thanks, Kenya. You saved my life!"

"Can you just go in there and chill for the night? The shit ain't over yet—believe that! We gonna have to answer for this shit sooner or later."

FACE FACTS

The rest of the way home Kenya's conscience started to kick in and go to work overtime. In a short amount of time she'd been involved in dancing, transporting drugs, covering up Swift's murder, disposing of Deacon's dead body, and now actually committing the act of murder herself. "I don't know how all this shit jumped off in the first place. All I was trying to do was make a little extra dough and get out the hood!"

Pushing the remote, she parked in the garage. Kenya, nursing the worst headache of her life, found her way to the couch and plopped down. The condo was quiet except the on-and-off sounds of Storm, strangely asleep in the basement, snoring. Kenya assumed that London was asleep also because it was so late. When her sister came walking down the stairs wide awake, it shocked Kenya.

"Oh, my God! I'm glad you're up. I need someone to talk to! This shit is important. Come in the kitchen with me."

London was thrown off that Kenya wanted her to come in the kitchen to talk. For some reason, she thought that the shit was about to hit the fan about her and Storm having sex on the floor by the refrigerator, so she sat at the table and braced herself for what was going to happen next.

Kenya set a plastic bag on the table and took her time pulling out the contents. The first two objects were both handguns. Especially alarming, one of them had obvious signs of blood on the handle. After what appeared to be a tape of some sort and a set of keys, the last thing Kenya quickly snatched out the bag was a designer purse.

"What is all of this?" London scanned the table, puzzled, as she watched her sister break down in tears.

Kenya went on to explain exactly what events took place earlier, from the moment she and Paris left the dinner they'd all shared together to now. By the time Kenya was finished with her confessional story, London was caught up in her feelings. She was pissed, infuriated, enraged, disappointed, and downright mad as a motherfucker at her twin for what she'd done in the name of friendship.

"Sis, why in the world would you do something so stupid?"

"Chocolate Bunny was gonna shoot Paris. What else was I supposed to do London, huh? You tell me."

"Listen, Paris had no business coming in Alley Cats acting all tough! That would have been on her! She brought whatever was gonna happen on herself!"

The twins' arguing went on and on until London, frustrated, got up from the table to make some coffee and slightly lost her balance, falling toward the stove.

"What's wrong with you?" Kenya suspiciously asked with her eyebrow raised. "You've been real clumsy lately. What's that all about?"

PARIS

"What took you so long to come home?" Paris screamed at the top of her lungs. "Was you out shopping for baby clothes and shit?"

"What in the fuck is your crazy-ass talking about now?" O.T. stood in the doorway, not in the mood for a shouting match.

"I already know about you and that trick having a baby, so don't try to deny it!"

"What female you talking about now, Paris—which one?" he asked, dismissing another one of her wild accusations.

"That lowlife tramp Chocolate Bunny, that's who!"

"You know what? I wasn't gonna tell you this bullshit cause it wasn't none of your damn nosy-ass insecure business, but you won't leave the shit alone!"

O.T., after months of being secretive about his late-night activities, filled Paris in. He explained the connection that he and Chocolate Bunny shared. Hearing the full and complete story left Paris in shock over what she and Kenya had done. Paris had no choice but to tell O.T. what had taken place and that Chocolate Bunny was dead, stuffed behind a Dumpster in the rear of Alley Cats.

His reaction was sheer anger as he sucker punched Paris dead in her mouth and left out of the apartment, telling her that he was never coming home or back to her troublemaking-ass again! A busted-mouthed Paris stumbled to the bathroom and opened the medicine cabinet. She twisted the top off a bottle of sleeping pills, swallowing a handful. After all the trouble she'd caused not trusting her man, O.T., she cowardly welcomed death, feeling that it was the only way out.

DAMN!

While Kenya poured the coffee in the mugs, London looked in Chocolate Bunny's purse to turn off her cell phone that kept ringing. There she found a thick, folded set of papers that were on the top and a few pictures. London read the first page of the legal documents, which were a purchase agreement for a house and couldn't believe her eyes. "I think you need to see this paper." She motioned to Kenya. "Now!"

"Oh, hell naw! It couldn't be! What the fuck did we do?" Kenya shouted out with remorse after reading the paperwork.

The papers were a deed to Chocolate Bunny's new house. They had her government name on them as well as another, Mr. Royce K. Curtis. The picture in her purse was an ultrasound that also had Royce's name on it. "All this time Royce's old ass has been the one she's been fucking around with? Why didn't she just say that bullshit? What was the big deal?"

Storm had waked up after getting a call from O.T and had been at the kitchen door eavesdropping and cut her off. "Because after the big fight you and Royce had down at Alley Cats about me, we thought it'd be better for you not to know that the old man was our new connect with some uncut product Javier had given him. Plus, it ain't really none of your business who Chocolate Bunny fucked with outside the club, O.T. or not."

"Storm, I—" Kenya tried to explain, knowing she had messed up once again.

"You know what, Kenya? From day one right off rip, I should've known that you was gonna be trouble. My little brother warned me about dealing with you, but I wouldn't listen. Now it's about to be a damn all-out street war because you and your sidekick Paris fucked the fuck up and killed that girl for nothing! The streets of Dallas gonna run red for this shit! I'm done with your ass for real this time! You costing me way too much!"

Kenya went into hysterics as she started throwing dishes against the wall and begging for Storm's forgiveness once again. Having no self-respect, the once Detroit diva was crawling on her knees, pleading with him not to leave her. London, stunned, was now pissed as she watched her own flesh and blood lower herself by this pathetic display.

"Kenya! Get up off that damn floor! His cheating-ass ain't worth humiliating yourself like this! Get up!"

"And as for you, bitch! I 'bout done had enough of your instigating-ass too! Why don't you pack your bags and get to stepping with her bad-luck-ass!" Storm ran up in London's face like he wanted to swing. "Get your funky-ass the fuck out my house!"

"Slow down, Storm! This is my sister's house too!" London fired back, standing her ground.

"Well, Kenya, you gonna tell this tramp to be ghost or what?" Storm waited with a smirk on his face. "It's me or her, and I'm not playing around this time!" It grew quiet in the room as all eyes were on Kenya, who was breathing hard, wiping the tears from her eyes. After a long pause she finally mumbled.

"What did you say?" Storm demanded to hear. "Speak up, we can't hear you!"

"I said, London, would you mind getting a hotel room somewhere until me and Storm figure all of this mess out?" Kenya, ashamed of what she'd just asked, failed to look at her twin sister. "Please, sis, it'll only be for a few days, I promise—until we work stuff out!"

"Naw—make that forever!" Storm shouted in response to Kenya's question to her sister.

"Oh, it's like that?" London was heated over what Kenya said. "I've put my life on hold for you for months and now you're taking his side over mine! How could you?"

"Please, London!" Kenya whimpered, not wanting to face or hear the truth. "Please!"

Storm started to laugh and couldn't help himself as he taunted his woman's sister. "You heard her now, didn't you? So go pack your shit and leave so I can get back to my life."

"Yeah, okay! Not at all a problem!" London headed up the stairs and to her room to gather her belongings. "You two deserve each other! I don't know how I stayed here in this madhouse this long anyhow!" she yelled as she tossed her clothes and a few personal items in a bag.

When she came back down Storm and Kenya were sitting on the couch talking. He was still dogging Kenya out, but stopped to sneer at London's seeming fall from grace. "Don't worry,

I already called your silly, jealous-ass a cab so you can just go wait on the damn curb!"

Kenya was silent as London passed by and went into the kitchen to get something else before struggling to drag her bags to the front door. Just as she opened the front door the cab was pulling up and blew once. London looked back at her twin, giving her one last chance to change her mind. "You sure about this, Kenya? You're picking this slimeball dope dealer over me?"

Kenya lowered her head in embarrassment over what was apparently her decision. After all she and London had been through and stuck together, the sisterly love and bond they shared was now being torn apart.

"Okay, so you know what it is, bitch! Now kick rocks!" Storm held the door open. "And don't bother us again! Kenya will call you, so don't call her, you lonely ho!"

London was really overjoyed to leave. She'd suffered through just about enough of Storm's disrespectful mouth, not to mention Kenya's spineless demeanor. With all her bags on the porch she spitefully turned around to face her sister and the man she'd so easily chosen over their bond. Vindictively, London pulled up her T-shirt, exposing a secret of her own that would shut a boisterous Storm up once and for all. Rubbing her slightly pudgy stomach in a circular motion, looking down, London grinned, delivering the showstopping revelation of the evening thus far.

"It's all good this way. Don't worry about me. And trust, I ain't gonna be lonely for long, believe that!" London smirked as all eyes were on her, rubbing her belly. "Tell your *Aunt Kenya and Daddy Storm* bye!"

"I don't understand! What the fuck are you talking about, London?" Kenya broke her silence, running over to the door, following her sister out to the cab. "What you mean, *Daddy Storm*? What is you talking about?"

Getting inside the cab, London shut the door and rolled down the window. "Ask his ass what happened in the kitchen that night!" She pointed at the condo where Storm was standing, face buried in his hands, having a flashback. "He knows." London then instructed the cab to pull off, leaving Kenya and Storm on the doorstep arguing. Smiling, she opened one of her bags, which contained both guns and Chocolate Bunny's purse.

"Where to, Miss Lady?" the driver inquired.

"Yes, can you please take me to police headquarters—the Homicide Division? I need to drop something off!"

I guess blood ain't thicker than water!